The Tale Of

PRINCE
VESSANTARA

The Tale Of
PRINCE VESSANTARA

A NOVEL BY

ASHIN SUMANACARA

Library and Archives Canada/Government of Canada

The Tale of Prince Vessantara/Ashin Sumanacara

Includes illustrative paintings.

Paperback Book ISBN 978-1-7782016-3-9

Electronic Book ISBN 978-1-7782016-4-6

Audio Book ISBN 978-1-7782016-5-3

SUBHASHITA BOOKS

3381 Boul. Dagenais O.

Laval, QC, Canada. H7P 1V5.

www.sumanacara.com

PREFACE

Welcome to 'The Tale of Prince Vessantara,' a timeless classic from ancient Pali literature, cherished throughout Southeast Asia. This story, considered one of the most important and celebrated Jataka tales in the Theravada tradition, recounts the life of Prince Vessantara, whose journey of selflessness and compassion has inspired generations of readers, regardless of their beliefs or backgrounds.

This novel is a retelling of the Vessantara Jataka, drawing from its various adaptations. It follows the Great Being, Prince Vessantara, blessed with great wealth and prosperity, as he faces trials and tribulations that lead him to embody the noble qualities of a Bodhisatta. His unwavering generosity and selflessness remind us of the importance of putting others before oneself. The story is a profound exploration of sacrifice, love, and generosity.

The inspiration for this book came from my fascination with the tale of Prince Vessantara and the lessons it teaches us about compassion, sacrifice, and the human condition. The writing process involved extensive research into the cultural and historical contexts of the tale, aiming to preserve its authenticity while making it accessible to modern readers. Through this adaptation, I hope to convey the richness and beauty

i

of the cultural traditions from which it originates and to inspire a broader audience.

This book aims to inspire, entertain, and enlighten readers. It is my hope that the story of Prince Vessantara will move you, make you think, and leave a lasting impression on your heart and mind. As you immerse yourself in the world of Prince Vessantara, may you find inspiration in his journey of self-discovery, love, and ultimate redemption.

I want to express my heartfelt gratitude to you, dear reader, for taking the time to read this novel. I hope it brings you as much joy, profound emotion, and inspiration as it has brought me.

Ashin Sumanacara,
PhD in Buddhist Studies (Mahidol)

PROLOGUE

In a kingdom far beyond the mountains, there lived a prince named Vessantara. Born into a life of luxury and privilege, he had every comfort and pleasure at his fingertips. But this story is not about his lavish lifestyle or royal bloodline. It is about his journey from the heights of power to the depths of poverty, from the love of his family to the sacrifice of his own happiness.

The tale begins with the ten blessings bestowed upon Phusati by Indra, the ruler of the thirty-three gods in Tavatimsa heaven. Phusati, Indra's favorite consort, was requested to be reborn as a human princess. She would become the wife of King Sanjaya of Sivi and the mother of the future Bodhisattva. And so, a child was born—a child who would grow up to be Prince Vessantara.

From a young age, Vessantara was given a white elephant with a magical rain-making ability, ensuring fine crops in the kingdom. But when Brahmins from the nearby kingdom of Kalinga begged him to give them the elephant to save their own land from drought and famine, Vessantara showed his generosity by granting their request. This gift, however, angered the people of Sivi. They convinced the king to banish his son, and thus, Vessantara, along with his wife Maddi and their children, set out into exile.

Their journey led them through forests, encountering ordinary folks, hermits, and beggars, each testing their resolve and challenging their notions of generosity and compassion. But it was one particular man, an old Brahmin named Jujaka, who would change the course of their lives. Desperate for servants to perform his domestic work and please his young wife, Jujaka begged Vessantara to give him his children. In a moment of selfless sacrifice, Vessantara granted his request.

Vessantara's beloved wife, Maddi, was blocked from returning to the hermitage by disguised deities. When Indra appeared as a Brahmin to request Maddi as a gift, Vessantara's ultimate sacrifice was put to the test, and the fate of his family hung in the balance. Will Prince Vessantara be able to overcome his desires and fulfill his destiny as a Buddha-to-be? Can love and compassion triumph over greed and selfishness? The answers lie in the pages of this timeless tale.

The tale of Prince Vessantara and his journey of self-discovery, love, and devotion has captivated readers for centuries. It is a tale of sacrifice, generosity, and the ultimate test of faith. It reminds us that true happiness lies not in material possessions but in the love and compassion we show to others.

This novel will capture your heart and leave you pondering its profound message long after you turn the last page. Follow Vessantara's journey as he faces the greatest challenge of his life and emerges as a true hero and embodiment of selfless giving.

CONTENTS

Chapter 1

Tenfold Boons

Once upon a time, in the enchanting kingdom of Sivi, there was a king named Sivi who ruled over the city of Jetuttara. The city lay nestled among rolling hills and fertile plains, blending prosperity with tranquility. The sun would rise each day, casting a warm golden glow over the landscape, promising another day of abundance.

The governance system, a source of great efficiency, ensured that peace and harmony prevailed, filling the atmosphere with the delightful laughter of satisfied people. Expansive fields extended as far as the eye could see, adorned with plentiful crops that murmured stories of agricultural abundance.

In the heart of this prosperous kingdom, skilled artisans plied their crafts with unmatched mastery, gracing temples and houses with breathtaking brick and stone artwork. The streets, decorated with structures displaying artistic brilliance, intertwined flawlessly throughout urban and rural areas, uniting them in a symphony of culture.

For the tired traveler, each street corner in the kingdom provided a haven of rest, complete with clay water jars as symbols of hospitality.

Among the fields, a beautiful symphony of crops, vegetables, and vines created a lush green canvas that seemed to infuse life into the earth. The woodland groves, with branches heavy with ripe and juicy fruits, invited those seeking solace in the embrace of nature.

***

The Sivi King had a son named Sanjaya. The prince was a source of immense pride and joy for the King. However, as Prince Sanjaya grew into a young man, the King began to worry about his future and the fate of his kingdom after he was gone.

Determined to ensure his son's happiness and the kingdom's prosperity, the King searched far and wide for a suitable bride for Sanjaya, who was not only beautiful but also wise, kind, and compassionate.

After an exhaustive and lengthy search, the King finally found the perfect match for his son. He brought a princess named Phusati, who was the daughter of King Madda, to Jetuttara to introduce her to Sanjaya.

Phusati was a stunning beauty with a sharp wit and a kind heart, and it was not long before the prince was utterly smitten with her.

The King held a grand ceremony after making arrangements for Sanjaya and Phusati's marriage. During this event, the Princess was crowned as the new ruler of Jetuttara and was gifted the entire kingdom. As a result, the King stepped down from his throne, passing on the crown to his son's bride.

During her reign as Queen, Phusati won the hearts of Jetuttara's people with her beauty, intelligence, and compassion, resulting in a flourishing kingdom.

***

During a certain period of time, a teacher named Vipassi emerged in a far-off land. He was distinct from others due to his profound understanding of the human condition and unique perspective on life. Vipassi stayed in the deer park of Khema near the bustling city of Bandhumati, where his teachings began to spread far and wide. He became famous for his wisdom, and many sought after his teachings.

While King Bandhuma was staying in the deer park, he received a message from another king who brought a valuable gift. The gift consisted of a golden wreath and precious sandalwood. The King who sent the gift was impressed with Vipassi's teachings and wanted to show his appreciation for all the outstanding work Vipassi had done for his people. It was a sign of respect for this great teacher.

Vipassi was grateful for the gift, but remained focused on his teachings. He continued to guide his disciples and share his knowledge with anyone willing to listen. His teachings were profound and resonated deeply with those who heard them.

***

Two stunning Princesses lived in a magnificent and luxurious palace, enjoying lavish and splendid lifestyles. The palace was adorned with intricate designs and ornate decorations, making it a true masterpiece of architecture. The Princesses, adorned in sparkling jewels and flowing gowns, mesmerized all who crossed their paths with their grace and elegance.

The elder sister was wise and gentle, while the younger one was clever and skilled with her hands. One day, they heard about an elder monk named Dasabala, who had dedicated his life to teaching and spreading the dharma. Filled with reverence for the monk, the sisters decided to offer him a gift. They sought permission from the King to visit Dasabala at his hermitage in the deer park, and the King agreed.

Two Princesses began a journey to the hermitage. Upon their arrival, they were amazed by the great teacher Dasabala and felt a strong sense of devotion and respect towards him. The elder Princess carried a golden box filled with sandalwood powder, while the younger Princess held a golden necklace made from the wreath gifted by the King. They had come to offer their prayers and express gratitude for the teacher's wisdom.

The elder Princess gently sprinkled the sandalwood powder over the golden body of Dasabala, uttering a prayer for a future where she could be the mother of a Buddha like him.

The younger Princess gently placed a gold-laced necklace around Dasabala's neck, praying it would remain until she achieved sainthood. Dasabala was pleased with the gesture from the sisters. He prophesized that the elder sister's prayer would be fulfilled and that she would one day be the mother of a great Buddha.

After leaving the hermitage, the Princesses felt blessed and humbled by their experience. However, they were unaware that their prayers would be answered in ways they could never have imagined. The wisdom they had gained from Dasabala would guide them through the trials and tribulations yet to come.

***

Two sisters made a noble sacrifice that deeply impacted their lives. After their passing, they found themselves in the world of gods. The elder sister traveled between the world of gods and humans. It is said that at the end of the ninety-first age; she was reborn as Queen Maya, who later became the mother of the Buddha.

In the meantime, the younger sister also traveled between these worlds. Legend has it that during the time of Dasabala Kassapa, she was born as the daughter of King Kiki. She was an extraordinary sight to behold from the very moment of her birth. The young girl had the appearance of a golden necklace on her neck and shoulders, so exquisite that it seemed as though a painter had created it. The King named her Uracchada, "adorned with a necklace."

When Uracchada was just sixteen years old, she lived a luxurious life as the daughter of King Kiki. One day, she heard the words of the Master and was deeply moved by their piety. This spiritual awakening propelled Uracchada to embark on a journey of self-discovery that would have a lasting impact on her life.

Uracchada was inspired by the teachings of the Master and felt motivated to dedicate her life to pursuing enlightenment by joining the Order. She made the decision to take her vows and become a nun on the same day that she achieved the fruit of the First Path.

As Uracchada continued her spiritual practice, she gained more wisdom and understanding. She devoted hours each day to meditation, seeking to comprehend the true essence of existence and uncover the mysteries of the universe. Eventually, she achieved a spiritual insight that few had ever reached.

***

King Kiki of the kingdom of Kikisavati had eight daughters, whom he cherished dearly. He gave each of his daughters a unique name that held a special meaning in his heart. The eldest daughter was named Samani, which meant "wise woman." The second daughter was named Samana, which meant "peaceful one." The third daughter was known as Sister Gutta, signifying her spiritual purity and devotion. The fourth daughter was named Bhikkhudasika, which meant "follower of the monk's teachings." The fifth and sixth daughters were named Dhamma and Sudhamma, respectively, meaning "righteousness" and "pure righteousness." Lastly, the seventh daughter was known as Samghadasi, meaning "one who serves the community."

All of King Kiki's daughters were renowned for their beauty, intelligence, and kindness. They devoted their days to meditation, studying the teachings of Buddha, and performing charitable acts for others. King Kiki was immensely proud of his daughters and had faith that they would one day make a positive impact on the world.

Among them, Phusati became Sudhamma. She dedicated her life to performing good deeds and helping those in need. She was widely recognized for her kind and compassionate nature. One day, she learned about the teachings of the great Buddha Vipassi and was deeply touched. In order to pay her respects to him, she decided to present him with a gift of sandalwood. When Phusati presented a gift to Buddha Vipassi, he was pleased with her offering. Her generosity made her body anointed with fragrant sandalwood, bringing her peace and happiness. She continued to perform good deeds and give generously and eventually passed from the world of humans to the world of gods. Phusati's good deeds continued in the world of gods, and she eventually became the chief Queen of Sakka, the King of the gods.

***

Sakka ruled the celestial realms with divine splendor and regality. He was the embodiment of heavenly grace and majesty, surpassing earthly standards of physical beauty.

He stood with a noble posture, emitting a radiant and otherworldly glow that illuminated the heavenly abode with ethereal light. His complexion, reminiscent of the fullest moon, conveyed a sense of timeless purity. His eyes, deep pools of wisdom, reflected the cosmic knowledge he had gathered over eons. His benevolent gaze cradled both compassion and authority.

His face exhibited a timeless beauty that was untouched by the passage of time. His features conveyed a perpetual youthfulness that defied mortal comprehension. A calm smile graced his lips, expressing a sense of serene benevolence that welcomed the inhabitants of the celestial realm.

He was dressed in magnificent robes that shone with iridescent colors, reflecting the beauty of the cosmic universe. The fabric of his outfit flowed smoothly, resembling the flowing rivers of the celestial world and resonating with the harmonious rhythms of the cosmos. He was surrounded by a divine aura that pulsated with energy, casting a radiant glow that enveloped him in an ethereal radiance.

***

Sakka and Phusati had known each other for what seemed like an eternity. He had observed her growth and prosperity in the mortal world and had embraced her into the realm of the gods, appointing her as the chief queen. However, at present, he could sense that her time in heaven was nearing its end.

He observed the customary signs indicating Phusati's departure from paradise. He knew he must act quickly to ensure her peaceful journey to the afterlife.

He carefully escorted her to the Nandana grove, a place of unparalleled beauty. As they walked through the gates of the grove, they were greeted by a captivating aroma of exotic flowers. The garden was an oasis filled with lush trees and fragrant plants blooming in a myriad of colors. The gentle rustling of the leaves in the breeze created a serene melody that matched the enchanting beauty of the garden.

In the middle of the grove, there was a Mucalinda lake that was crystal-clear and surrounded by soft, velvety grass, which felt cool to the touch. Colorful birds flitted around the trees, and their sweet songs blended together in a symphony of sound that seemed to lift the soul.

The garden was a source of joy and delight for the gods. It was a place where they could forget their troubles and relax amidst the beauty of nature. As they strolled along the winding paths, they passed by groves of fruit trees that were heavy with ripe and juicy fruit. They also came across small ponds where fragrant lotus blossoms floated serenely on the water.

In this place of pleasure and tranquility, time appeared to halt, and anxieties dissipated. It was a realm of everlasting beauty, a sanctuary where the exhausted and the distressed could discover calm and satisfaction in the warmth of nature's embrace.

Sakka and Phusati arrived at the beautiful celestial Nandana garden, which was adorned with lush greenery and colorful blooming flowers. Upon reaching there, Sakka politely invited her to take a seat on an intricately designed chair, and he sat beside her. In a calm and authoritative tone, he spoke to her, saying, "My dear Phusati, it is my great pleasure to offer you ten wishes of your choice. You can ask for anything that your heart desires."

As Phusati contemplated Sakka's words, he smiled kindly at her. "I grant you ten boons of grandeur," he said. "Choose whatever brings you the most splendor."

Phusati expressed her gratitude for his kindness, but she was confused about her situation. She looked at Sakka and asked, "I am honored to be in the presence of such a distinguished ruler of the divine. However, I wonder what wrong I have committed to deserve to be uprooted from this beautiful place, like a tree blown away by the winds?"

Phusati, who was once lively and vibrant, was now filled with grief. Although she had lived a long and virtuous life, she felt sad in her final moments. He noticed her distress and spoke to her in a gentle voice, reassuring her that she had done nothing wrong and that she was still dear to him. He explained that her merit had been exhausted and depleted, which is why he was speaking to her.

Illustration 1: Lord Sakka, the King of the gods, bestows ten boons upon Queen Phusati.

Phusati looked up at him, her eyes filled with tears. "What can I do, my lord?" she asked. "I feel so helpless and alone."

Sakka held her hand and spoke in a soft voice. "Your time of departure is approaching, and the hour of death is near," he said. "However, I have ten boons that you can choose from before you pass away. Please choose one of them, Your Majesty." Surprised, Phusati asked, "What are these boons, my lord?"

Sakka smiled. "Whatever you desire, my dear queen," he said. "Choose any boons, and I will grant them to you."

Phusati listened intently to the words of Sakka, feeling a sense of despair washing over her. She knew that her time had come, and she had accepted her fate. However, he had granted her a boon, and she was filled with gratitude for his kindness.

Phusati knew exactly what she wanted. She asked for her first boon without hesitation: to spend the rest of her life in Sivi's realm. The peaceful and beautiful place brought her a sense of calm and contentment. She felt grateful for the opportunity to live out the rest of her existence in a realm she loved, even after her death.

Sakka attentively listened to Phusati's request and responded with a gentle smile. He believed he had made the correct decision by granting her the boon, as it would ensure that she spent her remaining days in peace and happiness. As Phusati closed her eyes, he observed her expression of gratitude for the beautiful life she had lived and the gift that had been bestowed upon her. When she opened her eyes again, she felt a sense of weightlessness and liberation engulfing her. She knew that her time was drawing near, but she was content with the realization that she had lived a virtuous life and that she would be able to spend the rest of her days in a realm that she cherished. Phusati was resolute in her decision to make the most of the ten wishes granted to her by Sakka. She had already asked to live out her life in Sivi's realm.

However, there was something else that she wished for dearly. It was something that she had always been self-conscious about - her appearance, especially her eyes. She longed for her eyes to be black, with pupils like that of a fawn and black eyebrows. Without hesitation, she spoke to Sakka, "May my eyes be black, with pupils like a fawn, and my eyebrows also black. Let my name be Phusati, and may this be my boon, O generous one."

Sakka listened attentively and nodded his head in agreement. He could see the sincerity in Phusati's request and felt it was a small thing to grant. With a wave of his hand, he granted her the boon she had requested.

Phusati was overwhelmed with joy and gratitude as she realized she now had the eyes she had always desired. As she looked around, everything seemed more vibrant and beautiful than ever before. Phusati knew that she had made the right choice in selecting this gift. She felt a sense of confidence and pride in herself. She felt beautiful, and she was at peace with herself for the first time in a long time.

Queen Phusati felt incredibly grateful for the boon bestowed upon her. She now had the motivation to live her life to the fullest and positively impact those around her. She was determined to be the best version of herself and use her gift to its fullest potential. Sakka's generosity had touched her heart deeply, and she knew that this moment would stay with her forever. Phusati closed her eyes and spoke softly, her voice barely above a whisper. She said, "Grant me a son, O generous one, and let him be revered by kings. May he have a fame and glory that stretches beyond the boundaries of our realm. Let his heart be filled with compassion and generosity, and may he always listen to the prayers of those around him."

Her heart was filled with happiness as she spoke her third wish. She longed for a son who would be a source of pride for the kingdom, a ruler adored and respected by all. She wished for him to be renowned for his courage, distinguished by his achievements, and captivating in his demeanor.

But, more importantly, she wanted her son to have a compassionate and generous heart. She hoped that he would always be willing to listen to the cries and prayers of his people. She wanted him to rule with fairness and kindness and to always strive to do what was right, even if it was difficult.

The thought of her son brought a smile to her face, and she momentarily forgot about her impending death. She closed her eyes and imagined the child she would soon have, playing with his toys in the palace gardens, surrounded by the love and adoration of his people.

Upon opening her eyes, she felt a warmth spread through her body, as if a comforting presence surrounded her.

Sakka listened to her words, and a knowing smile crossed his face. He knew that Phusati's wish would be granted, and a great ruler would be born from her womb. He silently blessed the child and promised to watch over him throughout his life.

Phusati's request for a worthy son warmed the hearts of those who heard it, and whispers of the unborn Prince's greatness began to spread throughout the land. The people eagerly awaited the prince's birth, anticipating the day when he would take his place as the ruler of their kingdom.

Phusati was proud of her figure and didn't want her pregnancy to change it. The thought of feeling sluggish and heavy with a child made her uncomfortable. She had heard of other women whose pregnancies had caused permanent changes to their bodies, and she was determined not to suffer the same fate.

She made her next request: "Oh, King of the gods, please allow my figure to remain slender and graceful like a finely crafted bow while the baby is in my womb."

Sakka listened attentively to Phusati's request and smiled. He understood how crucial it was for a mother to feel beautiful and self-assured during pregnancy. With a wave of his hand, he granted her request, assuring her that her figure would remain as graceful as ever.

Phusati wondered how Sakka, the King of gods, could make this possible, as pregnancy was a natural process and couldn't be altered even by a god.

However, she trusted in the power of Sakka's boons, and she knew that he would not grant her something that was impossible. She took comfort in the fact that her baby would be born to a mother who was still beautiful and graceful and that the experience of childbirth would not scar her body.

Phusati closed her eyes and whispered a prayer of gratitude to Sakka for his kindness and generosity. As she opened her eyes, she felt a sense of peace and calm wash over her. She knew that everything would be alright and that the future held great promise for her and her family.

A graceful and slender figure during Phusati's pregnancy and a son who would receive the love and respect of all. But now, she yearned for something more intimate, something that would make her feel beautiful and alive even in her last moments.

"Grant me this boon, O generous one," she said, her voice trembling slightly. "May my breasts remain firm and my hair not turn white, with an unblemished body that can release the condemned."

God Sakka looked at her with compassion in his eyes. He could see the pain and fear in her heart, the knowledge that her life was coming to an end. He knew that this boon was not just about physical beauty but about dignity and grace in the face of death.

"Your request is granted, Phusati," he said gently. "May you have the strength and courage to face the end of your life with the same grace and beauty that you have shown throughout it."

Phusati felt a rush of gratitude and relief wash over her. She knew that Sakka had granted her every wish and that she would spend her final days in comfort and happiness. With gratitude, she thanked him, then left, feeling a sense of contentment and peace that she had not felt in a long time.

Phusati sat in the heavenly garden, surrounded by the soft sounds of water lapping at the shore of the nearby lake. She took a deep breath and closed her eyes, feeling the warmth of the sun on her skin and the softness of the grass beneath her feet. She felt truly blessed, for she was in the presence of Sakka, the ruler of the heavens.

"My Queen," said Sakka, "Several boons have already been granted. What is it that you desire next?"

Phusati opened her eyes and looked at Sakka, a sense of reverence and awe filling her heart. She took a deep breath and spoke, "Your Majesty, I am grateful for the many blessings you have bestowed upon me. But I long for something more, something that will fill my heart with joy and contentment. I wish to be surrounded by the cries of herons and the calls of peacocks, with attendants who are as beautiful as they are skilled. I wish to hear poets and bards singing our praises, with shawls waving in the air as a sign of their appreciation."

Sakka listened attentively to her request and nodded his head. "So be it," he said and smiled.

Phusati sat in deep thought next to Sakka, longing for the one thing she had yet to receive despite receiving many boons from him.

She took a deep breath and spoke from her heart, "Dear King, I am grateful for all that you have granted me over the years, but there is one thing that I long for. When the servant calls out loudly at the painted door, 'God bless King Sivi! Come to dinner!' I wish to be recognized as his queen and acknowledged in every aspect of our lives together."

She wanted to be acknowledged as the Queen of Sivi in every aspect of their life together. Although it might seem insignificant to some people, to her, it was a symbol of the respect and honor that she deserved as the wife of the great King Sivi.

Sakka listened attentively to Phusati's request and nodded his head in agreement. "So be it," he said, flashing a warm smile. Phusati, who was standing before the King of gods, felt an overwhelming sense of gratitude in her heart. She had been blessed with ten boons, each one a valuable gift from the heavens. She could feel the weight of these boons, heavy with promise and possibility, as she stood there in awe."

My lady bright, your ten wishes shall be granted in the beautiful Sivi kingdom where your heart's desires will come true," said Sakka.

Sakka continued to speak and said, "The mighty king of gods, Sujampati, also known as Vasava, spoke these words with immense joy. He granted a boon to Phusati. Sujampati recognizes the potential within you and desires to see you prosper and flourish in the Sivi kingdom."

Phusati felt immense gratitude and bowed her head deeply, moved by the gods' kindness and generosity. She knew that the gift she had received was rare and precious and one that she would forever cherish. As she closed her eyes, the beauty and majesty of the Sivi kingdom appeared in her mind's eye, calling out to her and beckoning her to come.

CHAPTER 2

VESSANTARA'S BIRTH AND THE
MAGICAL WHITE ELEPHANT

After receiving ten boons from the King of the gods, Phusati left the heavenly realm and entered the human world. She found herself in the womb of King Madda's Queen, where she grew and developed in a state of pure bliss.

As the time for her birth approached, a sweet and pleasant fragrance filled the entire kingdom. It was an aroma they had never experienced before, and the people were amazed by it. They knew that something miraculous was happening, and they eagerly awaited the arrival of the child, who was said to be blessed by the heavenly gods themselves.

When Phusati was born, her body was filled with a sweet sandalwood fragrance that filled the room and left everyone in awe. Her parents named her Phusati, which means "blossoming." As many attendants raised her, Phusati became a beautiful young woman. Her grace and charm captivated all those who saw her. Even as a child, she had a natural beauty that radiated from within, and as she grew older, her beauty only became more refined and alluring.

At the age of sixteen, Phusati was known for her unparalleled beauty, which became the talk of the entire kingdom. Her beauty was so mesmerizing that even the gods were overwhelmed with joy, and many suitors traveled from far and wide to seek her hand in marriage.

***

One day, Phusati received news that the King of Sivi's son, Prince Sanjaya, was to be granted the white umbrella, a sacred symbol of peace, power and authority. Furthermore, the Princess of Jetuttara had been invited to be his bride. The news filled Phusati's heart with a sense of awe and wonder as she eagerly accepted the invitation, excited at the prospect of becoming a queen.

As Phusati made her way to the city of Sivi, she felt a rush of excitement and anticipation, wondering what lay ahead for her. Upon reaching the palace, she was greeted by Prince Sanjaya, a noble and handsome young man whose eyes lit up with joy upon seeing her.

They married in a grand ceremony, surrounded by their families and friends. As a result of their union, Phusati became the Queen consort of Sivi and had a court of sixteen thousand women to attend to her needs. Phusati embraced her new role with grace and dignity, using her beauty and charm to bring joy and happiness to the people of Sivi. She was known for her kindness and revered by all.

Sanjaya, the young King of Sivi, had always known that his wife, Phusati, was an extraordinary woman. From the moment they met, he had been struck by her beauty and gentle spirit, and he knew he had found his true love. Their love grew stronger as time passed, and they were blessed with many happy years together. Phusati's love grew stronger, and they were blessed with many happy years together.

Phusati had a desire that had yet to be fulfilled. Though she had been granted nine boons by the King of gods, Sakka, her deepest desire for a son had yet to come to pass.

The King of gods, Sakka, had been observing the couple's love and devotion, and he, too, wished for Phusati's desire to be fulfilled. And so, he resolved to make it come true for her.

With great care and attention, Sakka set about fulfilling Phusati's tenth and final boon. He called upon the gods of fertility and abundance and poured all of his divine power into making Phusati's dream a reality.

***

In the Heaven of the Thirty-Three, Sakka, the King of the gods, was deep in thought. He had just realized that the time of the Bodhisatta's residence in heaven was coming to an end.

The Bodhisatta, a being of extraordinary virtue, had taken residence in the heavenly realms, driven by a noble purpose. His goals transcended the fleeting pleasures of celestial existence. Instead, he aspired to cultivate perfections, weaving a tapestry of virtues that would illuminate the path toward enlightenment.

In the celestial expanse, the Bodhisatta's aims extended beyond personal salvation. He sought to perfect the ten perfections (paramita) — a sacred journey encompassing generosity, moral conduct, renunciation, wisdom, energy, patience, truthfulness, determination, loving-kindness, and equanimity. Each perfection was a stepping stone towards the ultimate goal of Buddhahood, a state of supreme enlightenment for the benefit of all sentient beings.

Bodhisatta aimed not only for personal liberation, but also for the enlightenment and liberation of all beings across the realms. The heavenly abode, with its temporal joys and delights, had been a platform for the Bodhisatta to fulfill his sacred commitment to the path of enlightenment.

***

As Sakka contemplated the situation, he knew what had to be done. He approached the Great Being, Bodhisatta, and respectfully addressed him, "Your Honor, it is time for you to go to the realm of humans. You must be conceived in the womb of Phusati, the Queen consort of the King of Sivi."

The Great Being, who had been meditating, opened his eyes and looked at Sakka with surprise. "What do you mean, king of gods?" he asked.

Sakka explained, "Phusati, the Queen of Sivi, has prayed to me for a godly son. I have granted her nine of the ten boons she desired, but the tenth is the most important. I have decided to grant her wish by sending you to be conceived in her womb."

Bodhisatta nodded in agreement, understanding the significance of Sakka's words. "I understand, King of gods. I'm ready to be born as Phusati's son in the human realm."

Sakka smiled and said, "You are indeed a Great Being. Undoubtedly, you will fulfill your mission with honor and dignity. May you be born with all the wisdom and compassion of your previous lives."

King Sakka had requested the sixty thousand gods destined to be reborn. He had asked them to be reborn as children of King Sanjaya's courtiers in the mortal realm.

The Great Being, Bodhisatta, descended from the heaven of the Thirty-Three and was conceived in the womb of Queen Phusati. At the time of Bodhisatta's conception, the sixty thousand gods were also conceived as the children of the courtiers in the kingdom.

***

Queen Phusati was a woman of great compassion and generosity. She felt a responsibility to aid those in need, especially since the Great Being was growing inside her.

One day, as she sat in her chamber, she decided to make a request to her husband, King Sanjaya, to build six alms halls in the city, one at each of the four gates, one in the middle of the city, and one at her door.

In order to make sure the alms-halls were adequately funded, Phusati planned to distribute six hundred thousand pieces of currency a day. This was a significant amount of money, but she was determined to do whatever it took to ensure that the poor and needy in the kingdom were taken care of.

King Sanjaya was delighted by his wife's plan and consulted the fortune-tellers about the child in her womb. The fortune-tellers declared that the child would be a giver of charity who would never grow weary of generosity. The news pleased the ruler, and he continued to be generous, as had been his habit.

In the kingdom of Sivi, the conception of the Great Being had brought immense prosperity to the land. The benevolent aura of the King had attracted the attention of monarchs from all over India, who began to bestow him with lavish gifts.

Sanjaya, the King of Sivi, grateful for the good fortune that had befallen his kingdom, became even more generous. He established hospitals, monasteries, and temples throughout his kingdom, where he provided free healthcare and education to his people.

The reputation of the King's generosity spread far and wide, and soon, people from all over India began to flock to his kingdom to receive his blessings. The King welcomed them all with open arms and never turned anyone away empty-handed.

***

The sun was setting over the vast kingdom city of Vessa, casting a warm glow over the bustling roads of the capital. A group of travelers had just arrived in the heart of the city, led by Phusati and her husband, King Sanjaya. They had been traveling for days through treacherous terrain and harsh weather to reach this important destination.

Phusati, who was heavily pregnant, had a swollen belly carrying the future ruler of Vessa. The King was worried about his wife's well-being, but they could no longer delay their journey. They had to be in the capital for the birthing ceremony, which would take place in a few days.

While traveling through the quiet roads of Vessa, she suddenly clutched her stomach in pain. The King quickly took charge and called for his advisors to find a suitable place for his wife to give birth.

The group quickly made a birthing room. The room was ready within minutes, and she was taken inside to begin the labor process.

The King was anxiously waiting outside the birthing room, pacing back and forth. He was used to leading armies and guiding his people during times of war, but at this moment, he felt powerless and vulnerable. All he could do was wait for updates on the condition of his wife and child. Time seemed to pass slowly, and he couldn't shake off the feeling of unease that was eating away at him.

Eventually, after what felt like an endless wait, a midwife appeared from the room, holding a small bundle in her arms. The King hurried towards her, his heart beating with excitement. The midwife smiled at him, revealing a tiny, wrinkled face from beneath the blankets.

She held out the baby to him and said, "It's a boy, Your Majesty."

The King felt a surge of pride and joy as he looked down at his newborn son. He took the baby into his arms, cradling him gently as tears welled up in his eyes. He knew that this child was the future of Sivi, the one who would carry on his legacy and lead their kingdom to greatness.

***

The Great Being Bodhisatta emerged from his mother's womb, fully formed and with his eyes wide open. The midwife who had assisted in his birth was stunned. It was unlike anything she had seen before. The baby didn't cry like newborns usually do, but instead, he calmly looked around with a serene expression.

His mother, who had just gone through a long and difficult labor, was exhausted. She lay back on the bed, trying to catch her breath, when she heard her baby's voice. She initially believed it was just her imagination, but then she heard it once more.

"Mother, can I give you something? Is there anything I can do for you?" The baby's voice was clear and strong, and his tiny hand reached out towards her.

His mother was amazed. She had never heard of such a thing happening before. When she gazed into her baby's eyes, she witnessed an understanding and wisdom surpassing his age.

She smiled and said, "My dear child, you have already given me the greatest gift of all - your presence. I am so grateful for you."

The Great Being looked at his mother with a sense of compassion and love. He realized that she was tired and wanted to make her life easier. So, he reached out his hand again and said, "Mother, let me help you."

His mother was surprised by her baby's words, but she was also moved by his concern. She nodded, and The Great Being softly held her hand. He closed his eyes, and she felt a warmth emanating from his little body.

Suddenly, her tiredness dissipated, and she felt renewed energy coursing through her veins. She felt a sense of peace and contentment that she had never experienced before.

The Great Being opened his eyes, and his mother noticed a brightness and light in them that she had never seen in anyone else. She realized that her child was unique and had a special destiny.

**

When the Great Being Bodhisatta was born, he let out a powerful cry that echoed through the halls of the birthing chamber. His parents were amazed by the strength and clarity of his voice, and they knew that he was destined for greatness.

As they held their newborn son, he proclaimed three times that he had arrived. His parents were taken aback by his display of confidence. They knew their son was unlike any other child they had seen.

***

As word of the birth of the new Prince rapidly traveled throughout the vast kingdom of Vessa, a surge of ecstasy and happiness reverberated through every corner of the land. From the bustling streets of the cities to the quiet countryside, people were filled with joy and elation at the news of the royal heir's arrival. The lively streets of Vessa were transformed into a vibrant celebration, alive with the rhythmic beats of drums and the melodic strains of Indian instruments.

The bustling city was alive with energy as its people, adorned in colorful and eye-catching garments, converged in the central square. The flickering glow of the oil lamps cast a serene and calming aura, providing a peaceful respite from the chaos of everyday life. The air was thick with the sound of joyous laughter and the unique hum of merriment that echoed through the hills. The sweet perfume of jasmine and marigold flowers wafted through the air, creating a pleasant and alluring fragrance that enveloped the senses, making it impossible not to feel completely and utterly transported by the beauty of the moment.

As the sun started to dip below the horizon, the festive atmosphere in Vessa grew more vibrant. The air was filled with the soulful tunes of traditional Indian instruments, including the dhol, khartal, khol, pakhavaj, nagara, and flute, played by musicians sitting cross-legged on ornate carpets. The melodious strains of the sitar echoed through the air, creating a harmonious tapestry that enveloped the celebration and amplified the joyous spirit of the occasion.

Dancers, dressed in colorful silks, whirled and twirled to the rhythmic beats, their feet creating a symphony of sounds against the cobblestone streets. The intricate footwork of Ghoomar dancers reflected the grace and elegance of the royal celebration. A group of musicians played the mridangam, filling the air with pulsating beats that set the pace for the dancers' graceful movements.

Amidst the lively music and dance, the aroma of local delicacies wafted from street-side stalls and royal kitchens. The air was filled with the rich and alluring aroma of kheer, a sweet dish that had been flavored with fragrant saffron and the warm spice of cardamom. On the table, it shared space with savory samosas and an array of delectable sweets, including jalebi and laddoo, each one tempting and delicious in its own right.

The magnificent royal palace, adorned with intricate tapestries and gleaming oil lamps, served as the focal point of the festive celebrations. Dressed in their finest attire, the King and queen joined their subjects in the festivities. Court musicians entertained the gathering with classical ragas, while the Queen, overwhelmed with joy, performed a traditional dance that captivated the audience.

The kingdom of Vessa celebrated the birth of their Prince for several weeks. The streets were filled with joyous music, the air pulsated with dance rhythms, and the aroma of delicious food lingered, creating a festive atmosphere that engraved this auspicious moment into the hearts of all who witnessed the joyous birth of the royal heir.

***

During the day of Bodhisatta's naming ceremony, the village elders came together to give a name to the newborn. But, surprisingly, the Great Being spoke up and informed them that his name had already been given.

"My name was not given by either of my parents," he proclaimed. "I was named Vessantara because I was born on Vessa Street."

The elders were surprised by the revelation that the child had named himself, as it was unprecedented. However, they could not ignore the confidence and authority in the voice of the Great Being, and they agreed to respect his wishes. When the baby cried for the first time, a female flying elephant appeared from the clouds above, carrying a young white elephant as a gift. The people were amazed by the sight, as they understood that this was a symbol of great luck and blessings to come.

The King, a wise and just ruler, was overjoyed by the arrival of the Prince. He spared no expense to ensure the child's proper care. He assigned four times sixty nurses, all chosen for their height and beauty, to provide the Great Being, Prince Vessantara, with sweet milk and nourishment.

Meanwhile, the white elephant named Paccaya grew alongside the Prince, serving as his loyal companion and protector. The two were inseparable, and the people of Vijitapura whispered that the bond between them was a sign of the Great Being's divine nature.

***

The King was overjoyed with the birth of his son. However, this was not just an ordinary birth, as on the same day, sixty thousand other children were also born. This remarkable occurrence was seen as a sign of good fortune and abundance, and the King spared no expense to ensure that all the children received proper care.

Each and every child was cared for by appointed nurses, who provided them with love and nourishment. The King's son grew up surrounded by friends and companions amidst this sea of children.

To honor and present his son, the King crafted an extravagant necklace made up of a hundred thousand pieces of money. It was a symbol of his love and affection, a token of his pride in his son's birth.

But the Prince, being only four or five years old at the time, was not interested in such material things. He saw how hard his nurses worked to care for him and the other children, and he knew that they deserved the necklace more than he did.

And so, without hesitation, the Prince decided to distribute the necklace among his nurses, saying that he wanted to share the gift with them. He distributed the necklace among his nurses, refusing to take it back despite their protests.

The nurses were overwhelmed by the Prince's gesture and tried to return the necklace, insisting that it was too valuable for them to accept. However, he was adamant and refused to take it back, saying that it was a token of his gratitude for their love and care. The nurses, touched by his benevolence, finally accepted the necklace with tears of joy in their eyes. They knew that they were caring for a very special child indeed.

***

Word of Vessantara's selfless act spread quickly, and it reached the ears of the King, Vessantara's father. King Sanjaya was impressed by his son's kindness and appreciated his gesture, saying that it did not matter who gave the gift. He then decided to have another necklace crafted as a replacement for the one Rajat had given away.

When the Prince received the second necklace, he again distributed it among his nurses, who were amazed at his generosity. They had never seen such a kind-hearted Prince before. Prince Vessantara continued to give away the necklaces to his nurses again and again, nine times in total.

Each time, the nurses were moved by his kind-heartedness and tried to refuse, but the Prince insisted, saying that he owed them everything for their care and love.

***

The young Prince, Vessantara, lay on his couch, lost in thought. He was only eight years old, but he had a mature and profound understanding of the world. As he lay there, a sudden realization dawned on him – he wanted to give something of his own, something that truly belonged to him.

Vessantara had always been a kind and generous child, but he felt that his gifts were not enough. He wanted to offer something that would truly satisfy him, something that would come from the depths of his heart. The thought of giving away a piece of himself filled him with a strange sense of excitement.

As he lay there, lost in thought, Vessantara's mind raced with possibilities. What could he give that would truly satisfy him? Suddenly, a thought struck him – he could offer his heart to someone who needed it. The mere thought of it sent shivers down his spine.

"If one were to seek out my heart, I would tear it from my chest and offer it up," Vessantara whispered to himself. The idea of giving away something so precious, so integral to his being, filled him with a sense of awe and wonder.

Prince Vessantara's thoughts continued to race. "If my eyes were requested, I would unhesitatingly pluck them from their sockets," he said, his voice barely above a whisper. "If I were asked for my flesh, I would not hesitate to part with all of it."

Prince Vessantara's words were not just empty promises. He knew deep down that he would do anything to help those in need, to give of himself without hesitation. His heart swelled with a sense of purpose, and he knew that he was destined for greatness.

Prince Vessantara, even at a young age, was known for his generosity and intellect. Despite his privileged upbringing, the prince often felt a strong longing within him. He yearned to understand the true nature of the world and the meaning of existence.

***

One day, Prince Vessantara decided to engage in a profound meditation to seek answers to his burning questions. He closed his eyes, taking a few deep breaths to find his inner calm. He felt the gentle breeze of the air and the warmth of the sun on his skin, allowing his body to relax while his mind cleared. He opened his eyes and found his focus, beginning to meditate deeply.

Vessantara allowed his mind to drift, exploring his inner self and the world around him. His thoughts were focused on the enormity of the planet, on the vastness of the universe that surrounded him. He visualized the earth, a massive entity that spanned forty trillion leagues in breadth and two hundred thousand leagues in depth.

As he meditated, Prince Vessantara felt the earth beneath him tremble as if it were a great, crazed elephant. The ground quaked and thundered, and he could sense the power and magnitude of the planet. Even Sineru, the highest of mountains, appeared to bend and sway like a sapling in the wind as if it were dancing and leaning towards the city of Jetuttara.

Vessantara's meditation was so intense that it seemed to affect the very elements of nature. The sky was filled with thunder and lightning, and the sea churned and roiled like a pot of boiling water. It was as if the whole universe was in an uproar as if some great force was at work.

Prince Vessantara remained calm and centered, his mind focused on his meditation. He knew that he was witnessing something extraordinary, something beyond human understanding. As he continued to meditate, he saw the King of the gods, Sakka, clap his hands in approval.

And then, something even more extraordinary happened. The great Brahma himself gave a signal of agreement. It was as if the whole universe was in an uproar, responding to the Prince's thoughtful meditation.

The Prince experienced a state of deep reflection and found himself lost within it. His mind was consumed with thoughts of charity and the act of giving.

Despite his young age, he felt a strong desire to make a difference in the world.

As thoughts and ideas swirled in his mind, he was suddenly overcome by an intense feeling of compassion and empathy. It was as if a switch had been flipped, and all of his senses were heightened by the suffering of those around him. At that moment, he knew that he had to do something to make a difference.

Without hesitation, Prince Vessantara declared, "I would willingly give anything and everything to help those in need. I would give my blood, my body, my heart, or even my eyes if someone were to ask for them. My commitment to helping others is unwavering and absolute." As the words left his lips, he felt a sense of peace wash over him. He knew that he had made a promise to himself and to the world that would never be broken. From that moment on, he knew that his purpose in life was to help others and make a positive impact. He decided to devote himself to charity work as he believed it was the best way to make a real difference in the lives of those who needed it most.

Prince Vessantara felt a renewed sense of purpose and determination as he opened his eyes. He was determined to make a difference. He had finally discovered his true purpose in life, which was to assist those who were in need. And he knew that with his unwavering commitment to the act of giving, he would be able to do just that.

***

One day, while standing on his terrace, a thought occurred to Prince Vessantara: "What I give is not from me, and it does not satisfy me; I would like to give something of my own." With this realization, the Prince began to contemplate the act of charity and giving.

As he delved deeper into his thoughts, the Prince declared to himself that he would willingly give his blood, body, heart, or eyes to anyone who asked for them. Such was his genuine declaration, a testament to his unwavering commitment to compassion and selflessness.

At sixteen, Vessantara, a Prince known for his wisdom and intelligence, had completely mastered all the sciences. His intellect was unparalleled, and his knowledge was vast. He was revered by all who knew him, and his fame had spread far and wide, and his father, King Sanjaya, was immensely proud of his son's accomplishments.

***

One day, King Sanjaya summoned the Prince to his court, accompanied by his mother and the royal family. The King had a grand plan in mind - he wanted to make his son the King and ensure a prosperous future for the kingdom. After much discussion, the royal family decided to bring Maddi, the Prince's first cousin, to be his Queen consort. Maddi was known for her grace, kindness, and beauty, and the King believed that she would be the perfect match for his son.

The news of Princess Maddi and Prince Vessantara's engagement spread like wildfire throughout the kingdom of Sivi. The King had made the official announcement, and when the news of their engagement broke, the entire kingdom erupted in celebration. The nobles were overjoyed, and the common folk were thrilled to witness such a momentous occasion.

***

Princess Maddi had always dreamed of finding true love, but she never imagined that it would come in the form of Prince Vessantara. The moment she heard that he had agreed to marry her, her heart felt as if it had burst with joy. She felt an overwhelming excitement, like a thousand butterflies taking flight in her stomach.

As she walked through the palace halls, she felt as if she was floating on a cloud. She saw beauty and wonder everywhere she looked, and she knew that her life would never be the same again. She had found her Prince, and together, they would start a new life filled with love, happiness, and bliss.

Along with Princess Maddi, they brought sixteen thousand female attendants, all of whom would serve as the Queen's retinue.

Standing in front of the grand entrance of the palace, she saw Vessantara waiting for her. He looked dashing in his royal attire, and she couldn't help but feel a surge of love for him. He took her hand and led her down the aisle as the guests cheered and clapped.

When they finally reached the altar, Maddi looked into Vessantara's eyes and saw nothing but love and devotion. She knew that she had found her true soulmate, and she felt so blessed to have him in her life.

The kingdom of Sivi was abuzz with excitement as preparations were underway for the grand marriage ceremony of Prince Vessantara and Princess Maddi. People from around the kingdom eagerly anticipated the event and gathered in large numbers to witness the union of the Prince and the Princess.

As the ceremony began, the air was filled with the fragrance of flowers and the sound of hymns being sung. Vessantara and Maddi exchanged garlands, followed by the tying of the holy thread, signifying their eternal bond. They then exchanged their vows, pledging to be with each other for eternity.

Maddi was overwhelmed with a sense of calm and contentment as she basked in this moment of pure joy. Her heart swelled with gratitude as she realized that she was right where she belonged - in the arms of the man of her dreams, ready to embark on a new life together. She expressed her deepest thanks to the King and Queen for allowing their union to take place and knew that she and her husband would forever cherish this momentous occasion.

***

The noble Prince Vessantara was sprinkled with holy water, signifying his ascension to the throne. As the religious ceremony was completed, the coronation ceremony of Prince Vessantara began. He was presented with the royal insignia, a crown, and a scepter and was proclaimed the new ruler of the kingdom of Sivi. The crowd erupted in a loud cheer, celebrating Vessantara's accession to the throne.

The newly crowned King and Queen then embarked on a procession around the kingdom, waving at the cheering crowds who showered them with flowers and blessings. The procession ended with a grand banquet, and no expense was spared. The palace was adorned with flowers and lit up with a thousand candles. The air was filled with the melodies of musicians, and the scent of delicious food wafted through the halls.

Nobles from far and wide attended the banquet, dressed in their finest attire. The common folk were also invited, as the King and Queen wanted to share this moment of joy with all of their subjects. The atmosphere was electric with excitement and anticipation, and the love that filled the air was palpable.

The marriage and coronation ceremony of Vessantara and Maddi was a momentous occasion for the kingdom of Sivi. The entire kingdom was filled with joy and happiness as they celebrated the union of their beloved Prince and Princess. The royal family received praise and congratulations from all the attendees. They would now rule the kingdom together, spreading love, harmony, and peace throughout the land.

***

The newly crowned King, Vessantara, was overwhelmed with gratitude and responsibility. He felt grateful for the trust and confidence placed in him by his father and the people, but he also felt a sense of responsibility weighing heavily on his shoulders. He knew that he had been entrusted with the welfare of his people. He was determined to be a just and compassionate ruler who would prioritize his subjects' welfare above all else.

Upon ascending to the throne, the young King immediately displayed generosity and compassion towards his people. He was fully aware of the plight of the less fortunate in his kingdom and determined to make a difference in their lives. He believed that true leadership meant not just ruling with authority but also being a pillar of support and care for those in need.

One of the ways in which King Vessantara expressed his generosity was through charitable donations. Every day, without fail, he would provide six hundred thousand coins to those in need. He set up a system where people could come to him and request assistance, and he made sure that no one was turned away empty-handed. He would listen to their stories, offer them comfort and counsel, and provide them with the resources they needed to survive and thrive.

**

The kingdom erupted in joyous celebration as Maddi welcomed her newborn son. Maddi lay exhausted but elated, her newborn son cradled in her arms. She gazed down at the tiny, wriggling bundle, amazed by the power of the love that surged through her. This child, born to Vessantara and Maddi, represented their unity and promised the future of their kingdom.

The attendants bustled around her, their excitement palpable as they prepared to welcome the new Prince. A golden hammock, symbolizing his royal lineage, was quickly assembled, and the baby was gently placed inside. She watched with pride as her son was lifted high, surrounded by the shimmering gold.

News of the birth of the royal heir spread like wildfire across the kingdom. Temple bells rang out, heralding the news to all who could hear. The royal family was showered with gifts and blessings from all sides. People danced in the streets, and there was a feeling of jubilation everywhere. The kingdom was alive with the joyous celebration of a new life.

Maddi conceived a child as the young Prince grew up and learned to walk. In the royal palace, young Prince Jali took his first hesitant steps. His mother, Maddi, watched with pride as her son explored the world around him with his mop of curly hair and bright, curious eyes.

***

One day, as Jali was perfecting his newfound skill of walking, Queen Maddi went into labor once again. Her labor was intense, and the palace was filled with tension and excitement.

Finally, the cries of a newborn baby filled the air. The Queen had given birth to a daughter. The baby was carefully wrapped in beautiful black skin, a unique and striking feature that set her apart from everyone else. She named her Kanhajina, a name that soon became synonymous with beauty and strength.

The young Prince looked up to his sister with awe and admiration, and together, they were a formidable pair, each complementing the other's strengths. As the Prince and his sister grew, they developed a strong bond. Their bond only grew stronger with time, and they were the pride and joy of the kingdom.

***

Prince Vessantara forged a profound connection with a majestic creature of unparalleled beauty – the white elephant. A sight to behold, it stood with an aura of regality, its gleaming tusks curving gracefully, a testament to its noble lineage.

This magical elephant possessed an imposing size that commanded reverence. Its sheer presence evoked a sense of awe. The creature's radiant and smooth ivory tusks reflected the sun's gentle light, casting an ethereal glow upon the surrounding landscape.

Wherever this extraordinary being tread, a divine connection with the heavens seemed to unfold. The clouds above would heed its silent call, and with every step, the skies would open up, blessing the earth below with life-giving rain. It was as though the white elephant held the key to the very essence of nature, a celestial custodian ensuring the flourishing of the land it graced.

As the creature moved through the kingdom of Sivi, the people, in humble admiration, would gather to witness this wondrous spectacle. The air would be filled with a palpable sense of reverence, and the sound of hushed whispers acknowledging the magical presence of the white elephant would ripple through the crowd.

The creature's eyes were like profound wells of wisdom and tranquility as if they held the mysteries of the universe. Its majestic gait carried a quiet strength as if it bore the weight of the world with grace and humility. Upon witnessing this awe-inspiring being, the people of Sivi felt a strong bond with the divine forces that governed the natural world.

The white elephant, a celestial guardian in earthly form, became a symbol of prosperity and benevolence. Its association with rainfall bestowed upon it a revered status, a bringer of life and abundance to the kingdom.

***

Every month, Vessantara would embark on a journey that would take him to his six alms-halls. These were places where he would offer food and other necessities to those in need, a gesture of kindness and generosity that endeared him to the people of Sivi.

Vessantara traveled in style, riding on his superb white elephant. It carried Vessantara effortlessly, as its strong legs covered the ground quickly.

The King and his majestic white elephant were revered as they traveled from one alms-hall to another. People would come from miles around to catch a glimpse of Vessantara and his noble companion. They would offer prayers and blessings, hoping to receive a measure of his wisdom and grace.

For Vessantara, these journeys were more than just a simple act of charity. He treasured the chance to create meaningful connections with the people of Sivi. He felt for their struggles and rejoiced in their triumphs.

***

In a land not so distant, nestled beside the rolling hills and ancient forests, there thrived a kingdom known far and wide as Kalinga. As the scorching sun beat down relentlessly upon the kingdom of Kalinga, the once lush fields withered and turned to dust. The earth cracked and groaned under the weight of the unrelenting drought that had gripped the region. The people of Kalinga, once proud and self-sufficient, were now reduced to beggars, scavengers, and thieves.

The kingdom had been suffering from a severe drought for months, leaving the land barren and the people in despair. Despite their prayers and offerings, the rain gods seemed unwilling to bestow their blessings upon them.

For months, they had endured the unyielding heat and the unending thirst. They had watched as their livestock perished and their crops withered away. Their once vibrant villages were now nothing more than ghost towns, filled with the desperate and the destitute.

In the midst of a dire situation, a new breed of criminal emerged. Men and women who had never before contemplated such actions now found themselves driven to steal and loot in order to survive. As a result, the streets of Kalinga were no longer safe, and the people lived in constant fear of being robbed or attacked.

Despite the chaos and despair, there were still those who held onto hope. They refused to give up even in the face of such adversity. These brave souls ultimately rose up against the drought and its terrible consequences, fighting to reclaim their land and their way of life.

***

The palace courtyard of Kalinga was alive with the sounds of people gathered from all corners of the kingdom. They came with a plea - to ask the King for help in the face of disaster. The fields were parched, the rivers were dry, and the people were struggling to survive in the midst of a drought that seemed unrelenting.

The King of Kalinga, a man of great wisdom and compassion, listened carefully as each spoke. He heard their cries of despair and their pleas for mercy. And when they had their say, he rose from his throne and walked amongst them, his eyes full of empathy.

"What is it, my children?" he asked softly.

The people looked up at him, their faces etched with pain and fear. They knew that their fate was in his hands, and they waited anxiously for his response.

Taking a deep breath, the King spoke with a voice that was both firm and gentle. "Good, my children," he said. "I will bring the rain."

The people gasped in amazement, scarcely daring to believe what they had heard. But the King's expression left no doubt in their minds. He was a man of his word, and he would do whatever it took to save his people from this calamity.

With a renewed sense of hope, the people began to disperse, each one carrying with them the King's promise like a precious treasure. They knew the road ahead would not be easy and the rain could still be coming for a long time. But they also knew that they had a leader who would stand by them through thick and thin, a leader who would move mountains to keep them safe.

As they made their way back to their villages and their homes, the people looked up at the sky with newfound confidence. They felt a stirring in their souls, a sense of unity and purpose that had been missing for too long. And they knew that whatever happened in the days to come, they would face it together, with the King at their side.

The King of Kalinga, a just and righteous man, had promised to observe the holy day and had committed himself to virtuous actions, hoping that the gods would bless his people with rain.

But as the days passed, the sky remained clear, and the heat grew even more unbearable. The King was distraught. He had done everything he could to appease the gods, but they still refused to listen.

Desperate for a solution, the King called upon his citizens to gather in the grand palace. With a heavy heart, he spoke, "My beloved people, I have remained true to my commitment to live an honorable life and have kept my promise to observe the sacred day. Unfortunately, I cannot bring the rain. What shall we do now?"

The King, known for his wise and just rule, called a council of his trusted advisors to seek a solution to the crisis. They deliberated for hours, considering various options and invoking divine interventions, but to no avail.

Finally, a voice spoke out from the crowd. It was a wise older adult who had seen many such droughts in his long life.

"Oh, your Majesty," he said. "If you cannot bring the rain, then you should send the Brahmins at once to the city of Jetuttara, where Vessantara - the son of King Sanjaya - resides. He is renowned for his generosity and is blessed with a magnificent magical elephant. Whenever this elephant goes, the rains follow. Ask for the elephant and bring it here."

The King was skeptical at first, but the desperation in the people's eyes convinced him to give it a try. He summoned the Brahmins to his presence and selected eight of them, providing them with the necessary provisions for the journey.

"Dear Brahmins," he said. "Proceed to Jetuttara and get Vessantara's white elephant. Bring it here, and we shall reward you handsomely."

The Brahmins embarked on their journey, determined to fulfill their mission to bring Vessantara's elephant to their kingdom. They traveled through rugged terrain, crossing rivers and mountains and enduring scorching heat and bitter cold.

***

Finally, after many weeks of travel, the Brahmins arrived in Jetuttara. They were weary and dusty, but they did not let their fatigue dampen their spirits. They sought out the alms hall, where the locals received them with kindness and hospitality.

The Brahmins spent their days in the alms hall, resting and meditating. They covered their bodies in dust and mud as a sign of their devotion to their mission. They ate simple meals of rice and vegetables and slept on thin mats laid out on the ground.

As the days passed, they grew anxious. They knew that time was running out, and they had to find King Vessantara's magical elephant soon. They consulted with the locals, seeking information about the elephant's whereabouts.

Finally, they learned that Vessantara's magical elephant was due to arrive at the alms hall on the full moon. They made preparations for the journey to the city's eastern gate, where they would seek out the elephant.

The Brahmins set out from the alms hall on the night of the full moon, their hearts pounding with anticipation. They made their way through the narrow streets of the city, their steps muffled by the sound of their sandals on the cobblestones.

***

The sun had just begun to peek over the horizon as King Vessantara arose from his bed, ready to embark on his daily visit to the charity hall. He moved purposefully, cleansing himself with sixteen vessels of fragranced water in a purification ritual.

After the cleansing, Vessantara sat down to break his fast with a light morning meal. He savored the taste of the food and the warmth of the sun on his skin, grateful for another day of life.

After finishing his meal, Vessantara proceeded to the stables, where his magnificent magical elephant waited for him. The elephant was adorned with elegant decorations and jewels that sparkled in the morning light.

With a gentle pat on the elephant's trunk, Vessantara mounted the beast and set off towards the city's eastern gate. He rode with a regal bearing, his robes billowing in the breeze as the elephant strode confidently forward.

As they approached the gate, Vessantara could see that the city was bustling with activity. Merchants hawked their wares in the marketplaces, and children played games in the streets. It was a vibrant and lively scene, and the King felt a deep sense of pride and satisfaction in his kingdom.

***

The Brahmins had traveled far and wide to fulfill their mission, but fate had not been kind to them. They had arrived a little late at the eastern gate, and Vessantara had already made his way inside the charity hall to distribute offerings.

Disappointed but undeterred, the Brahmins decided to regroup and come up with a new plan. They sought refuge on a nearby mound, from where they could observe the comings and goings of the King and his entourage.

As they sat there, watching and waiting, they couldn't help but feel a sense of awe and wonder at the spectacle before them. Vessantara was a true vision of majesty and power, radiating an aura of regal grace and authority that seemed to fill the surrounding air.

Despite their admiration for Vessantara, the Brahmins retained their mission. They knew that they had to be patient and persistent if they were to achieve their goal.

Hours passed as Vessantara and his retinue continued their activities in the charity hall. The Brahmins watched from their vantage point, taking careful note of everything that had happened. With time, the Brahmins grew increasingly anxious. Would they ever have the chance to meet the King and ask for his magical elephant? They knew that time was running out, and that they needed to act quickly to achieve their goal.

Finally, Vessantara emerged from the charity hall and made his way back to the palace. The Brahmins watched as he mounted his elephant and rode off into the distance, his retinue following closely behind.

With a sense of urgency, the Brahmins scrambled down the hill and made their way to the city's southern gate. There, they positioned themselves strategically, waiting for the King to pass by.

As they waited, the Brahmins rehearsed their plan. They knew that they had only one chance to make their request, and they had to make it count.

Finally, they heard the King's entourage approaching. Their hearts racing with excitement and anticipation, the Brahmins stood at attention, ready to make their plea.

As the King's mighty elephant drew near, the Brahmins stepped forward, their eyes fixed on the monarch. They spoke with a confidence and authority that belied their humble appearance, making their request with all the eloquence and passion they could muster.

Their hands outstretched in a gesture of reverence, the Brahmins raised their voices in unison, proclaiming, "May the noble King be victorious!" The words echoed through the air, resonating with a deep and abiding respect for the man they held in such high regard. For Vessantara was a paragon of virtue and generosity.

King Vessantara noticed these Brahmins who had just greeted him. They looked tired and travel-worn, with hairy arms, matted hair, stained teeth, and dusty heads. He could sense their yearning for something beyond what they had in life.

Without hesitation, the King drove his elephant towards them, eager to learn more about their mission. As the majestic animal came to a stop, he spoke with curiosity, 'O Brahmins, reaching out your hands in supplication, what is it that you seek?'

"Your Highness," one of them said, "we seek a precious thing. One that only you possess."

"What is it that you desire?" Vessantara asked, curious.

"A magical elephant," the Brahmin replied, "with magnificent tusks like no other, a majestic creature that can bring rain on the asking."

The Brahmins further explained that they had come from a neighboring kingdom, seeking the King's white elephant. They believed that the elephant had the power to bring rain to their drought-stricken land.

Vessantara listened carefully, and he felt a profound compassion for those who were suffering in the neighboring kingdom. He was prepared to offer any of his possessions, from the top of his head down, to help them in their time of need. With unwavering resolve, he knew that his own comfort was insignificant compared to the desperate cries of those in distress.

And so, he proclaimed, from atop the back of the majestic elephant, "I grant, without hesitation, the elephant that the Brahmins seek - this noble beast, fit for riding and equipped with fearsome tusks."

The Brahmins were overjoyed, and they thanked the King for his generosity. Vessantara felt a great sense of satisfaction in his heart.

Illustration 2: Prince Vessantara gifts his treasured white elephant, a symbol of rain and prosperity, to a group of Brahmins.

With a heavy heart, Vessantara ordered the elephant Paccaya to be brought before the Brahmins. He knew that parting with such a priceless treasure would not be easy, but he was determined to fulfill the Brahmins' wishes.

As the elephant was brought before the Brahmins, Vessantara watched with a mix of sorrow and awe. He saw the magnificent elephant, adorned with his precious ornaments, standing proudly. He then made another decision that would leave everyone in awe of his generosity. He ordered all the ornaments on Paccaya to be given to the Brahmins as a gift. The Brahmins were overwhelmed with gratitude.

The elephant was adorned with priceless ornaments, and Vessantara gave each and every one of them to the Brahmins. The ornaments on the elephant's four feet were worth four hundred thousand, those on his two sides were worth two hundred thousand, the blanket under his belly a hundred thousand, and so on. The total worth of all the ornaments was a staggering four and twenty hundred thousand.

Besides the ornaments, Vessantara gave the Brahmins five hundred attendants, along with the grooms and stablemen who had been caring for the elephant. The total value of the gift was beyond measure, and it included seven priceless things - the elephant, the jewels great and small upon the canopy, the jewels in his necklace of pearls, the jewels in the goad, the jewels in the pearl necklace about his neck, the jewels on his frontal globes, and the ornament for luck on his trunk.

The Brahmins were overjoyed at the King's generosity, and they departed with the elephant and all its belongings. As they were leaving, a great earthquake shook the ground, and other warnings followed. The people of Sivi were amazed by these events and knew that something truly remarkable had occurred.

***

The lively city of Jetuttara was alive with activity as the Brahmins at the southern gate were presented with the magnificent elephant. A sense of foreboding had descended upon the people, and many trembled with fear and uncertainty.

A huge crowd gathered around the Brahmins, their faces twisted with anger and confusion. "Why are you taking our elephant?" they cried out. "You are mounted on it! This is an outrage!"

The Brahmins stood firm, their expressions cool and detached. "The generous King Vessantara has donated this elephant upon us," they replied calmly. "We are merely fulfilling his wishes."

Despite their protests, the Brahmins proceeded to pass through the city, the enormous elephant trailing behind them. The throng of people followed close behind, their voices raised in angry protest.

As they made their way through the streets, the Brahmins remained stoic and unyielding, their faces impassive as they navigated the sea of humanity. The people of Jetuttara continued to cry out in outrage, their fists raised in defiance.

***

The gift of the magical elephant had caused a rift in the city, and the Brahmins' actions had only widened the divide. The people were left with a sense of betrayal and injustice, their faith in their leaders shaken to the core. It was a moment that would have far-reaching consequences, forever altering the course of Jetuttara's history.

The citizens of the capital of Sivi had always been proud of their traditions and customs. They were religious and revered the great and noble Vessantara as their protector and savior. But Vessantara's recent decision to give away the tremendous magical elephant created a rift among them.

Some saw it as a great honor, a sign of Vessantara's power and influence. But others were furious. They saw it as a betrayal of their faith and a violation of their trust. They expressed their rage through vehement criticism, accusing him of greed and selfishness.

***

The sound of the magical elephant being granted by the foster King was thunderous and powerful. It shook the town to its core, causing fear and panic. The earth quivered at the sound, seemingly protesting against the decision.

Vessantara, however, remained calm and composed. He knew that he had done nothing wrong and that his decision was based on the greater good. He had accepted the gift of the elephant not for his own benefit but for the benefit of the people. He believed that the elephant would symbolize unity and strength, bringing the people of Sivi together in times of need.

***

King Sanjaya stood before his people, his eyes fixed on the magnificent white elephant that was being prepared to leave the kingdom. His son, Vessantara, had made the decision to give away the creature, and the people were not pleased.

The people, from all walks of life, approached the palace gates, their hearts racing with anticipation. They had never dared to approach the King before, but the thought of losing the white elephant was too much to bear. As they entered the palace courtyard, they saw that many others had also gathered there. From the Prince and the Brahmin to the mighty and the meek, from the mahouts and attendants to the charioteers and soldiers, the country landowners, and all the Sivi folk, they were all there.

In a loud and unified voice, they cried out to King Sanjaya: "Your empire is in ruins, Your Majesty! Why must your son Vessantara part with the elephant, who is so beloved by all? Why must our savior, the mighty white elephant with its majestic tusks, be surrendered? It was always so skilled in selecting the best positions to win every battle!"

King Sanjaya listened intently; his brow furrowed with concern. He was aware that the white elephant was a symbol of power and strength, and losing it would have a profound impact on his people. But he also knew that his son had made the decision with the best intentions.

The majestic white elephant was a sight to behold, resplendent in its jewels and majestic yak-tail fan. Its tusks were long and gleaming, and its pure white coat shone in the sun. It was outfitted with grand trappings and an exquisite white parasol, fully equipped to be ridden by a King. Despite the value of his possession, Vessantara had willingly given it away, along with his mahout.

The people repeated their message, their voices echoing through the palace halls. "Providing food, drink, clothing, fire, and transportation is a suitable and appropriate gift for a Brahmin," they said, their words laced with urgency. King Sanjaya's eyes narrowed as he listened to their demands. He knew all too well the weight of the Sivi people's wrath.

"O King Sanjaya, a friend of the people," they continued, "can you explain why your son, Prince Vessantara, has given away our precious elephant?"

The King's chest tightened at the mention of his son. He knew Vessantara had a kind heart, but his actions had caused unrest among the people. King Sanjaya tried to choose his words carefully. "My son," he began, "has always had a generous spirit. He saw how much the Brahmin valued the elephant and believed it would bring him joy."

"But at what cost?" the people demanded. "That elephant was a treasure and belonged to our people."

King Sanjaya raised a hand, hoping to calm the crowd. "I understand your frustration," he said. "But my son acted with good intentions. He did not mean to cause harm."

"If you do not comply with the requests of the Sivi people," they warned, "it is likely that both you and your son will face the consequences."

King Sanjaya sat on his throne, his eyes narrowing as he listened to the Sivi people's request. The tension in the air was palpable, and he sensed that something terrible was about to happen. His mind raced with thoughts of his beloved son, Vessantara, and the dangers that threatened him.

King Sanjaya suspected that the Sivi people intended to harm Vessantara, and his heart ached with fear and anger. He could not bear the thought of losing his son, who was blameless and noble in every way. As the people spoke, he felt his resolve harden within him.

"My nation shall exist no more, and my realm shall cease to exist," he declared in a low and fierce tone. "I will not remove a blameless Prince from his rightful place, no matter what the people may say. He is my own son, and I shall not evict him from his position. Let my country cease to exist, and let my kingdom be no more, but my son shall remain in his rightful place."

King Sanjaya's words echoed through the hall, and the people fell silent. They knew that he was a man of great strength and determination, and they realized that they could not force him to do their bidding. He stood up from his throne, his eyes flashing with defiance.

"I will not bring any harm upon him, for he remains a virtuous man," he declared. "Killing him with a sword would be a disgrace and would cause great sorrow. My son Vessantara, how could I ever do such a thing?"

King Sanjaya's words hung in the air, and for a moment, there was silence.

The citizens of Sivi glared at the King, their eyes brimming with anger and frustration. They had come to demand justice and would not be placated so easily. "Exile is the only right punishment for his wrongdoings," they cried out in unison. Vessantara must be sent away from this kingdom and never be allowed to return."

King Sanjaya's face hardened as he listened to their demands. He looked around the room, trying to find a way to satisfy both the people and his conscience. He knew that his son, Vessantara, had made a grave mistake, but he couldn't bring himself to abandon him completely. "Let us not discount the will of the people," he finally said, his voice calm but resolute. "But let us also not forget that Vessantara is still my son. Let us grant him a single night of joy and contentment; then, we will send him away together. By the dawn of the morning, let us come together to fulfill the people's wishes and bid him farewell."

The citizens of Sivi reluctantly accepted Sanjaya's compromise, but their anger still simmered beneath the surface. As they exited the hall, rumors of disloyalty and fragility trailed behind them. The King watched them leave with a heavy heart, knowing his decision would be unpopular but believing it was the right thing to do. As he retired to his chambers for the night, he wondered what the future would hold for his kingdom and for his son.

As the people of Sivi agreed to the Sanjaya's proposal, Vessantara was allowed to stay for one final night before he would be exiled from his homeland forever. As the crowd dispersed, King Sanjaya couldn't help but feel a twinge of guilt for his decision. He knew that exiling his own son was necessary to keep his kingdom safe, but it didn't make it any easier.

Realizing he needed to deliver the news to his son, the King sought a trusted messenger to ensure that his message was delivered with the utmost care.

***

King Sanjaya's messenger, a trusted and loyal member of the court, stood before him, his eyes locked onto the monarch's face. "Your Majesty," he replied, his voice low and respectful. "I will go to the Prince with all haste and deliver your message. But tell me, what shall I say to him? How shall I ease his sorrow and quell his fears?"

King Sanjaya paused for a moment, his thoughts drifting back to the events that had led to this moment. He remembered the anger and frustration of the people, their voices raised in a chorus of accusations and demands. He remembered the pain in his own heart as he weighed the fate of his beloved son against the safety and security of his kingdom.

Finally, he spoke. "The citizens of Sivi are in an uproar, including the nobles, Uggas, Vesiyas, Brahmins, Mahouts, bodyguards, charioteers, and footmen. They have all gathered here to send Vessantara away, and it will be done at sunrise tomorrow.

"Tell him that I acted out of necessity to protect the people and the realm that I have sworn to defend. Tell him that I still love him and pray for his safety and happiness wherever he may go. And tell him that when the sun rises on the horizon, all will gather to bid him farewell. This will be his fate, but it need not be his final destiny."

The messenger nodded solemnly, his face etched with a deep understanding of the gravity of the situation. "I will tell him all this and more, Your Majesty," he said, bowing low. "And I will deliver your message with the utmost care and respect."

With that, he turned and made his way out of the throne room, his footsteps echoing through the empty halls of the palace. As he left, Vessantara stood alone, his thoughts turned inward as he struggled to come to terms with the painful decision he had made.

***

The messenger dispatched by the sovereign of Sivi was a man of great importance. He had served the King for many years and was renowned for his loyalty and intelligence. He rode atop an armed elephant adorned in fine jewelry and scents. The animal was a sight to behold, with its tusks glistening in the sunlight and its ears adorned with jeweled rings. The messenger was determined to deliver his message swiftly, and so he urged his mount to move with speed.

The messenger, having finally reached the court of Vessantara, was overcome with emotion. Despite his great respect for the sovereign, he knew he had to deliver the news that would break his heart. He fell to his knees before Vessantara. Tears streamed down his face as he spoke respectfully to his master. "Your Highness, I come bearing news from your father. The people of Sivi, including the nobles and commoners alike, are united in their anger and demand action against you. They will come together tomorrow, at the break of dawn, to see the Prince off and drive you away from the kingdom."

Vessantara was stunned and confused by the news brought by the messenger. How could his acts of kindness and generosity have led to such anger and resentment? He had always believed that giving was a virtue, a way to spread happiness and joy to others. But now, it seemed his actions only caused harm and bitterness.

He turned to the messenger with a mixture of sadness and frustration, "I cannot understand why they would turn on me like this. I only sought to bring happiness to those around me, to share my blessings with others. Why would they seek to cast me out for this?"

The messenger, his face full of sorrow, replied, "It appears that your gifts have been overly generous, my lord. The Uggas, Vesiyas, charioteers, and Brahmins were all angered by your kindness and viewed it as a threat to their own prosperity. Consequently, they managed to persuade others to turn against you and force you to leave."

Vessantara could feel his heart sinking as he listened to the messenger's words. He had always believed that all would appreciate his acts of kindness, but now he saw how wrong he had been.

Vessantara stood in silence for a moment, contemplating the gravity of the situation. He had always been a generous man, giving away everything he owned to those in need, and he sat upon his throne, surrounded by his courtiers and advisors. He couldn't understand their grievances. What had he done wrong? What offense had he committed? He turned to the messenger for answers.

"If someone were to request something of me," he said, "I would be willing to offer up my eye, my heart, and my hand, as well as any riches, diamonds, pearls, or other valuable adornments I have. I would not hesitate to give, as it is in my nature to bestow gifts. Even if the people around me wanted to exile me or take my life, I would still not deny them anything they asked of me. I could be cut seven pieces and still would not cease in giving."

Vessantara's words shocked the messenger who stood before him. His demeanor was so calm and collected despite the grave news that had just been delivered. It was as if he had already made peace with the fact that his people would drive him away. The messenger couldn't help but wonder what kind of person could be so willing to give away everything they had, even their own life.

As the Prince spoke, his courtiers stood by in awe, whispering to each other in hushed tones. They had never before heard their beloved Prince speak in this manner despite his well-known kindness and generosity. His words were full of conviction and selflessness, and it was clear that he was prepared to do whatever it took to help those in need.

Vessantara's words moved the messenger, and he couldn't help but feel a twinge of guilt. King Sanjaya had sent him to deliver a message that would only add to the Prince's troubles, and he knew that it was not his place to question his master's orders. But as he looked into the Vessantara's eyes, he saw something that he had never seen before - a deep and abiding compassion for all living beings.

Vessantara's resolve was unshakeable, and he seemed almost happy at the prospect of being exiled. To him, it was just another opportunity to give and share his abundance with others.

The messenger took a deep breath and looked at Vessantara. He had always been the bearer of difficult news, but this time, he spoke from his own thoughts rather than being commanded by the King or the people. "Your Highness," he began, "the Sivi people wish for you to travel to Kontimara, near the hill Aranjara, which is a common destination for exiles. I have been instructed to inform you of this."

Vessantara knew that his father had acted out of love for his people. He was taken aback by the request. He had always been generous and kind-hearted, but the thought of being exiled was not something he had ever considered. He had a deep love for his people and could not bear the thought of being separated from them. Nevertheless, he understood that it was his duty to follow the wishes of his people.

Vessantara's heart sank as he heard the news. He knew he had done no wrong. After a moment of silence, the Prince spoke. "Very well, I shall take the path of those who have wronged. But I cannot leave without giving something back to the people. Therefore, I would like to offer a generous gift of seven hundred. But I need one more day to prepare for this gift. I humbly request the citizens to give me this additional day. I will make the donation tomorrow and depart the following day."

The messenger nodded approvingly and declared, "This is the news I shall bring to the people." With that, he left the palace and journeyed through the city streets, his mind buzzing with thoughts of Vessantara's exile. He knew that the people of Sivi were deeply divided on the matter. Some were in favor of the Prince's exile, while others believed that he was being unfairly punished for a gift that he had given freely.

As he walked, the messenger thought about the Prince's words and was struck by the selflessness of his offer. He knew that it was rare to find someone who was so willing to give of themselves, even in the face of adversity.

Eventually, the messenger arrived at the marketplace, where he knew that the people of Sivi would be gathered. He took a deep breath and made his way through the crowd, his eyes scanning the faces of those around him.

Finally, he spotted a group of people gathered around a street vendor, discussing the news of Vessantara's exile. The messenger approached them, his voice clear and firm as he spoke.

"Good people of Sivi," he began, "I have come to you with news of Vessantara's exile. He has agreed to depart to Kontimara but has asked for one more day to make a generous donation of seven hundred."

The messenger paused, allowing his words to sink in. He could see the uncertainty in their eyes, the fear of the unknown. But he also saw something else: a glimmer of hope, a sense of possibility.

With those words, the messenger bowed and stepped back, allowing the people of Sivi to discuss amongst themselves.

***

As Vessantara retired to his quarters, he contemplated the task ahead of him. Tomorrow, he would give away seven hundred of his most prized possessions, including elephants, horses, chariots, and attendants. He knew it would be a challenging task to gather everything and prepare for the grand gift.

Turning to one of his trusted captains, he instructed him to make all the necessary preparations for the gift-giving ceremony. The captain nodded, understanding the gravity of the situation. He knew that this was not an ordinary gift and that the Prince would go to great lengths to fulfill his promise.

With the preparations underway, Vessantara bid farewell to his courtiers and retired to the abode of Maddi, his beloved wife.

Vessantara sat on the regal couch, looking at his beloved Maddi with a tenderness that betrayed the burden on his heart.

He spoke softly, "My dear Maddi, all the possessions I have given you - whether they be grain, gold, treasure, or precious stones - be sure to find a place to hide them away. It is your father's dowry that you must secure."

Maddi's eyes widened with worry as she listened to her husband. She was a beautiful, intelligent woman who always supported Vessantara's generosity and never complained. But now, the weight of their uncertain future was beginning to take its toll on her.

"My lord," she said, trembling slightly, "could you tell me where I should locate such a safe place for this treasure?"

Vessantara's eyes met hers, and for a moment, they held each other's gaze as if trying to find solace in each other's embrace. Finally, he spoke, "In the correct proportion, bestow your wealth in the form of gifts; there is no better place than this to store it, as I am well aware."

Maddi nodded, understanding what her husband meant. They both knew that their future was uncertain, and they had to trust in the power of giving. It was a philosophy that Vessantara had always believed in and one that Maddi had come to embrace as well.

As they sat together, lost in their thoughts, the room filled with a peaceful silence that seemed to soothe their troubled minds.

"Maddi, my dearest," Vessantara said, taking her hand in his own. "I know this will not be an easy path for you, but I have faith in your strength and goodness. Remember that you are not alone and that I will always be with you in spirit. And if, by some misfortune, no one desires to be your husband after I am gone, do not lose hope. You are a woman of great beauty and virtue, and I am sure you will find happiness in due time."

As Maddi listened to the Vessantara's words, tears welled up in her eyes.

Maddi looked into the Vessantara's eyes, feeling a knot of worry forming in her chest. The news of his exile from the kingdom had come as a shock, and now he spoke of a dangerous journey into the wilderness. She couldn't bear the thought of him facing the perils alone.

"Your Majesty, why have you uttered words you should not have?" Maddi questioned, her tone laced with concern, and tears streamed down her cheeks.

Vessantara took a deep breath, steeling himself to speak. "The people of Sivi have become enraged at me for giving away the magical elephant, so they are expelling me from the kingdom. I must make the offering of seven hundred tomorrow, and then I will have to leave the city on the day after," he explained.

Maddi's heart sank at his words. Even for a moment, the thought of being separated from her husband Vessantara was unbearable. And the idea of him wandering alone through a dangerous forest filled with predators was too much to bear.

"It is not fitting, my love, that you should go alone," Maddi said, her voice full of conviction. "Wherever you shall journey, I shall accompany you there. My dearest wish is to die with you if I may not be near, but if death is the only way I can remain by your side, then so be it."

Vessantara looked at her, his eyes filled with gratitude and love. "You are the true embodiment of devotion and loyalty, my dear Maddi," he said, his voice filled with emotion. "I cannot ask you to face such danger. The journey ahead is fraught with peril, and I could not bear to see you hurt."

Maddi's face hardened with determination. She declared, "I would rather set my heart on fire with a passionate flame, the strongest of its kind, than exist in a world where I am not with you." "To me, death would be preferable to a life without you. The elephant's mate is often seen nearby, traversing mountainous paths or dense forests, regardless of the terrain. In the same way, I will follow you with my children, no matter where you go, and you won't find us a burden to provide for."

The beauty of the Himalayas had always enchanted Maddi. She would sit for hours listening to stories of its beauty and wonder. It was her dream to one day see it with her own eyes, to feel the cool mountain breeze on her face and breathe in the fresh air that she had heard so much about.

As she sat holding Vessantara's hands and resting his head on her lap, surrounded by the rolling hills of her palace, she sang softly to herself. Her voice was sweet and melodious, carrying on the wind to the ears of those passing by.

Her words were accompanied by praise for the Himalayan region as if she had been there herself:

As you gaze upon your pretty lads,
And hear their laughter ringing through,
Beneath the greenwood boughs, you'll forget
The crown that once adorned you.

Your children adorned with flowers gay,
Their hearts light, and their voices sing,
In our fair home, you'll forget
The burdens that being a King can bring.

To watch your boys in frolic play,
With flowers they joyously bring,
In our fair home, you'll forget

The worries that make your heart sting.

As dancing children perform with glee,
Their garlands round them cling,
In our fair home, you'll forget
The weight of the scepter and the ring.

The elephant who roams with ease,
His age a wondrous thing,
Within the woodland, you'll forget
The troubles that the throne can bring.

As night descends and stillness falls,
The elephant takes the wing,
In the quiet dark, you'll forget
The battles that make your heart sing.

To hear the great elephant's call,
His herd to him they bring,
You'll hear his mighty trumpet and forget
The wars that once made you a King.

The woodland glades and beasts that roar,
All that your heart would sing,
Within your sight, you'll forget
The power that comes with ruling.

The river's rush, the fairies' song,
The mountains' echoes ring,
You'll hear their music and forget
The loneliness that being a King can bring.

The screech-owl's note from the mountain cave,
A lonely voice to bring,
You'll hear his cry and forget
The isolation that the throne can bring.

The rhino and the buffalo,
Their power and their sting,
The lion and tiger, you'll forget
The fears that come with leading.

To watch the peacock dance and spring,
His plumes a brilliant thing,
Before his hens, you'll forget
The expectations that come with the ruling.

To see the egg-born peacock spread his gorgeous,
feathered wing,
Before his hens, you'll forget
The pressures that the throne can bring.

The peacock's neck, a purple grace,
His dance a royal thing,
Before his hens, you'll forget
The expectations that being a King can bring.

When winter's chill upon the land,
The trees with flowers ring,
With their sweet perfume, you'll forget
The coldness that ruling can bring.

The winter blooms of plants so fair,
The bimbajala's fling,
The kutaja and lotus scent, you'll forget
The harshness that being a King can bring.

The winter forest blooms so rare,
The lotus king of spring,
All that you see, you'll forget
The challenges that come with ruling.

For in this fair home, your heart is free,

And in the joy of simple things,
You'll forget you were once a King,
And find the peace that truly brings.

As the sun began to set and the sky turned a deep shade of orange, Maddi finished her song. She sang of the beauty of the Himalayas and forest life, her voice rising and falling with each verse as if she were lost in the memories of her own dreams. Each stanza was more beautiful than the last, her voice full of passion and emotion.

Vessantara was in awe. He had never heard such a beautiful voice before, nor had he ever been so captivated by a place he had never seen. Maddi's voice was like magic, and he could not help but feel the emotions and feelings that she conveyed through her singing. He smiled, touched by the beauty of Maddi's song.

CHAPTER 3

TRIALS OF GIVING AND EXILE

As Queen Phusati made her way towards her son's chamber in a carriage, her heart weighed heavily with worry and uncertainty. She was on a mission to uncover what her son would do in response to the severe command that had been imposed upon him. When she arrived outside their chamber, she listened with rapt attention to the conversation that was taking place within. Her sorrow and anguish were palpable, and her lamentations were filled with tears and heartbreak. Every word she spoke was a testament to the depth of her pain and the enormity of the task she had set out to accomplish.

The Queen was inconsolable after overhearing a conversation between Maddi and her son. She grieved over their destiny and declared that she would instead drink poison, jump off a cliff, or even hang herself than witness the unjust exile of her innocent child, Vessantara.

Vessantara's unwavering devotion to helping anyone who sought his aid was truly remarkable. His selflessness and generosity were so widely recognized that even rival kings held him in high esteem.

She sat in her chamber with a heavy heart, listening to the sound of the carriage wheels as they clattered over the cobblestones outside. She knew that she must go and see her son, but the thought of what she might find filled her with dread.

Vessantara, her beloved son, had been ordered to leave the kingdom, and she feared that his departure would bring only sadness and pain. With a deep sigh, she rose from her seat and made her way to the carriage that awaited her.

Phusati's thoughts turned to her son's remarkable qualities as the horses trotted through the countryside. Vessantara was a kind and generous Prince who dedicated himself to helping all those who asked. Even his rival kings respected him greatly and spoke of him glowingly.

***

Vessantara and Maddi were discussing with the Princess. As soon as they saw the Queen, they stood up and bowed respectfully. She gave them a slight nod, her eyes filled with tears.

Queen Phusati's sorrow and anguish could be heard in her tearful lamentations. Vessantara's wife, Maddi, also joined in the lament, waving her arms around the Queen and shedding tears like rain, while Vessantara remained neutral but deeply saddened.

The Queen lamented their fate. She declared that it would be better to drink poison, jump from a cliff, or even bind a noose around her own neck than suffer the injustice of exiling Vessantara, her innocent child.

King Sanjaya and Queen Phusati, along with their family and friends, all held Vessantara in the highest regard, and yet, why did they still choose to exile him, an innocent man? What was the purpose of sending away this beloved figure, who had done no wrong?

Vessantara, for his part, was calm and collected in the face of this injustice. He knew that his exile was a test, a trial of his character and his faith in the goodness of the world.

Phusati, overcome with sorrow, left her son's chamber and went to find the King. She entered the throne room, her eyes red from weeping, and fell to her knees before him. "Oh, my lord," she cried, "I beg you not to cast out your son. If you do, your kingdom will surely fall, like mangoes dropping to the ground. The people will desert you like a wild goose with a broken wing that cannot find water."

King Sanjaya looked down at her, his expression grave. He knew his wife was right. He loved his son dearly, but he could not ignore the law. "Phusati," he said, "I do not want to exile our son, but I cannot ignore the people's will. They demand justice, and I must uphold the law. Vessantara must leave."

"But he is blameless!" cried Phusati, tears streaming down her face. "He has done no wrong. Why must he suffer for the mistakes of others?"

King Sanjaya's voice was solemn as he replied to Phusati's plea, "Though it is a difficult decision to make, I will adhere to my royal duty and send thy son, the people's beloved leader, to an exile far away, for it is more important to me than even my own life."

The King's words struck her like a thunderbolt. She couldn't believe what she had heard, and tears welled up in her eyes. She felt as if a sharp sword had been plunged into her heart. Her son, Vessantara, was her pride and joy, the epitome of kindness and generosity. The mere thought of him being exiled from the kingdom was unbearable to her.

Hearing the King's hard decision, the Queen felt her world had crumbled around her. Tears flowed down her cheeks uncontrollably, and she clutched at her chest, feeling as if her heart would break into a million pieces. She had always been a strong and stoic woman, but at that moment, she was reduced to a mere shell of her former self. Then she began to lament and mourn, saying:

"Once swarms of men escorted him,
With flags brightly flown,
Like blooming trees in forests deep,

Today he goes alone.

Fine yellow robes from Gandhara's shores
That once around him shone,
Or ruddy hues like sunset's beam:
Today, he goes alone.

Through royal chariot, litter, and elephant,
He once did roam,
But now Prince Vessantara
Must travel on foot alone.

Once perfumed by sweet sandal-scent,
Awakened by dance and song,
Now must he bear rough skins,
Axe and pot, and pingo along.

Why must they not adorn his form
With yellow robes of silk,
And with a dress of bark and grass,
Make the entrance to the ilk?

How can a King, exiled,
Wear the bark of the tree,
To clad in bark and grass,
How will the Maddi bear to see?

Maddi, who donned Benares fabrics
Fine and fair,
What hardship now must she endure of
Bark and straw so bare?

Once in a chariot or coach,
A Princess she did ride,
How can she go today by foot
With no place to hide?

In a blissful state, she used to stand
With gentle hands and feet:
How can this Princess, so divine,
Enter the dark woods discreetly?

Her gentle hands and feet were so sweet, her life in joy
did start: But now those beautiful shoes she wore
Have pained her with each step apart;
How can the lovely Princess bravely start her journey now?

Once, she would go arrayed in finery's midst
a multitude of fair maids:
How can that beauty's grace now walk through
The wilds so serene?

Once she heard the jackal's howl,
She would be filled with fright:
How can that timid loveliness
Now walk the meadows bright?

Fearful of Indra's royal reign,
She'd quail and quake and cower,
At hearing but an owl's hoot,
This timid one would cower.

Like a bird that surveys its empty nest,
Bereft of its young,
So when I see my place empty,
My heart will break and frost.

My anguish will be like an eagle's,
Its nest bereft,
So when I see that empty place,
My grief shall never rest.

Like crimson geese beside a lake that's drained,

My body shall wither, and
I'll mourn not to greet my child so great.

And if you expel from the kingdom,
My guiltless child,
Though I would cry in grief,
I'd think my life had ended.

My son, my dearest, my heart aches for thee,
As you walk alone, and no one sees.
With each step, I feel the pain you endure,
And the thought of your suffering makes my heart impure.

The memories of our past, so happy and bright,
Now, it seems like a dream, a distant light.
The once blooming tree, now withered and dry,
Our love that once blossomed, now withered and died.

The thought of you, exiled, fills me with pain,
As I imagine you wandering through the terrain.
With no royal chariot, no litter, no more,
But only your strength, your courage, your core.

Oh, my son, my love, my heart aches for you,
As you endure this journey, so long, so true.
I pray for your safety, your strength, your will,
To endure this journey and still reach your destiny.

And as for me, left behind in this kingdom so cold,
My heart aches with the memories of the past, so bold.
But now, like a bird, my heart feels bereft,
For without you, my dear son, my life has no heft.

***

Queen Phusati's heart was heavy with grief and worry. She couldn't imagine her son living a life of exile, away from everything he had known and loved.

Her sorrowful cries pierced the stillness of the palace as she mourned the news of her son's exile. Her ladies-in-waiting rushed to her side, their faces etched with worry and concern. Each one tried their best to comfort the Queen, but her anguish was too great.

As the palace women gathered around their Queen, they felt her despair emanating from her very being. The air was thick with a sense of grief and loss, and the women wept and hugged each other in a show of solidarity. It was as if the entire palace had been consumed by the Queen's heartache.

The children were the first to take notice of the commotion, their curious eyes peeking around corners and doorways. They watched as their mothers and older sisters wept openly, unable to comprehend the depth of emotion on display. The Queen's sorrow was contagious, spreading like wildfire among the palace women and children.

It was a scene of pure chaos, with women and children strewn about the palace floors, their tears falling like raindrops. They were the living embodiment of the Queen's suffering, and their presence only deepened her heartache and despair. The palace was consumed by the Queen's pain as if it had seeped into the very stones and walls of the grand building.

***

The dawn was breaking when Vessantara stepped outside of his palace; his heart was filled with an unquenchable desire to help those in need. He looked out at the people gathered before him, and his eyes filled with tears as he saw their suffering. Without hesitation, he made a proclamation, his voice ringing out clear and firm: "Let all who are hungry be fed, all who are thirsty be given drink, and all who lack clothing be given what they need. I will provide for your every desire."

The people were amazed at Vessantara's words, and many could scarcely believe what they heard. But Vessantara's generosity was unwavering, and he insisted that every person who came to him be given the utmost respect and hospitality. His servants rushed to and fro, bringing food and drink to the gathered crowds while the King himself stood in their midst, offering words of comfort and encouragement.

As the day wore on, King Vessantara's generosity continued to shine, and people came from far and wide to receive his help. He never once wavered in his resolve to help those in need, and his heart swelled with joy as he saw the happiness and contentment of those he had helped. For Vessantara, there was no greater joy than that of giving to others.

Now, Vessantara, the generous Prince, decided to donate seven hundred of his most valued possessions to the people of Sivi who deserve them. There excitement and anticipation in the air as the people awaited Vessantara's most valuable gift.

Seven hundred elephants, adorned with golden girths and trappings, were given away to the deserving people of Sivi. Each elephant was accompanied by a mahout armed with a spiked hook. The citizens were overjoyed, and cheers echoed throughout the city.

Next, Vessantara presented seven hundred horses of Sindhi and thoroughbred breeds, their glistening coats shining under the sunlight. Each horse was ridden by a brave servant with a sword and bow. The air was filled with the sound of neighs and clattering hooves.

Vessantara's generosity knew no bounds as he gifted seven hundred chariots, each pulled by a team of armored warriors, their flags fluttering in the wind. The vehicles were adorned with the hides of tigers and panthers, a display of grandeur and royalty. Every driver was armed with a bow, ready to serve their King until the end.

Vessantara continued his gifting with seven hundred women, standing in carts adorned with golden jewelry and beautiful garments that accentuated their delicate waists and bright smiles. The kine he gave were each furnished with silver milk pails, their gentle mooing and grazing creating a soothing atmosphere. Vessantara granted seven hundred male attendants to whomever he chose.

Word of Vessantara's boundless generosity echoed through the vast realm of Jambudipa like a divine melody, captivating the hearts of all who had heard. In their celestial abodes, the gods themselves could not help but take notice and dispatched a heavenly messenger to deliver the astonishing tidings to the kings ruling over the land.

As the messenger wove through the ethereal realms, whispers of Vessantara's benevolent acts spread, igniting a spark of curiosity and anticipation among the kings. Eager to witness the magnificence of Vessantara's giving firsthand, the rulers of Jambudipa summoned their Khattiyas, noble warriors renowned for their valor and loyalty, to embark on a journey to the realm of Vessantara.

Arriving in regal chariots, the Khattiyas stood as proud emissaries of their Kings, their hearts filled with a mixture of excitement and awe. They had been entrusted with the honor of receiving the precious gifts that Vessantara had bestowed upon the world.

With grace and humility, Vessantara presented the Khattiyas with abundant treasures, surpassing even their wildest imaginings. Among the priceless offerings were noble maidens, radiant in their beauty and adorned in garments spun from celestial threads. These high-born maidens, now symbols of unity between the realms, would grace the courts of the kings, becoming living testaments to Vessantara's unparalleled generosity.

However, Vessantara's benevolence extended far beyond the realm of royalty. The Brahmins, revered custodians of ancient wisdom, were not overlooked in Vessantara's grand design. They, too, received tokens of his boundless generosity, bestowed upon them with the utmost reverence and respect. The Vessas, diligent merchants who traversed the land in search of treasures, found themselves blessed by Vessantara's gifts, their hearts brimming with gratitude. Even the Suddas, humble laborers who toiled tirelessly to sustain their lives, were touched by Vessantara's compassionate spirit, receiving gifts that would lighten their burdens and kindle hope within their souls.

As the Khattiyas and their fellow recipients returned to their respective kingdoms, they carried with them not only material wealth but also a newfound understanding of the boundless capacity for generosity that resided within the human heart. The news of Prince Vessantara's selflessness and the far-reaching impact of his giving reverberated throughout Jambudipa, awakening a shared sense of gratitude and reverence among its people.

From the opulent palaces of kings to the humble dwellings of commoners, the people of Jambudipa united in celebration, their hearts uplifted by the noble example set forth by Vessantara. Amidst the harmonious melodies of joy and gratitude, they recognized the transformative power of generosity, understanding that by giving selflessly, one could illuminate countless lives and forge enduring connections across the vast tapestry of existence.

***

As twilight draped its gentle veil upon the land, Vessantara, driven by an unyielding determination, continued to bestow his gifts upon those in need. The stars began to twinkle overhead, casting a soft glow upon his noble countenance. With Maddi, his devoted wife, by his side, he returned to his childhood home, an exquisite chariot carrying them through the moonlit path. The anticipation of the reunion weighed heavily on his heart as he approached his parents' dwelling, yearning for their embrace.

As he stepped onto familiar ground, Vessantara's eyes met those of his father, King Sanjaya, the just, a man of unwavering principles and wisdom. Their gazes locked, silently conveying a myriad of emotions. With utmost respect, Vessantara greeted his father, his voice carrying the weight of the sacrifices he was about to make.

"My noble father," Vessantara began, his tone filled with reverence and determination, "I come before you today to inform you of my departure. Maddi and I, bound by an unbreakable bond, shall make our way to the treacherous Vamaka Hill." He paused, allowing the gravity of his words to sink in, aware that his father's understanding was crucial in this defining moment.

"With each passing day, the destiny of all beings unfurls, and yet their dreams remain unfulfilled. Their journey shall lead them to the abode of Yama, the god of death," Vessantara continued, his voice resonating with a sense of inevitability. He spoke not only of his own impending fate but of the plight of all living creatures, highlighting the profound implications of his actions.

The weight of condemnation rested upon Prince Vessantara's shoulders, a burden born from the very people he had sought to uplift through his boundless generosity. A flicker of remorse flickered within him, igniting a determination to atone for his perceived wrongdoings. "I stand condemned by my own kin, for I have given so much from my own hands. To seek redemption, I shall venture into the wilderness, where panthers roam freely," he revealed, the path he had chosen clear before him.

Undeterred by the prospect of adversity, Vessantara's unwavering spirit shone through his words. "No matter how deep I sink in the mire of tribulations, I shall remain steadfast in my pursuit of goodness," he declared, his voice infused with a resolute resolve. His commitment to righteousness was unwavering, a beacon of light that pierced through the darkness that threatened to engulf his path.

Vessantara's gaze turned tenderly towards his mother, a wellspring of love and gratitude swelling within his heart. The depth of their connection was profound, forged through countless moments of care and nurturing. With utmost respect, he approached her, his voice carrying a gentle yet unwavering resolve.

"My beloved mother," Vessantara began, his voice laced with affectionate reverence, "the time has come for me to bid you farewell. Here I stand, an exile, cast out from the realm I once called home, burdened by the weight of perceived misdeeds. Though I gave away my possessions with the utmost compassion, my people have deemed me guilty and exiled me from these familiar lands."

As he spoke, the ache of separation mingled with the flickering ember of determination within Vessantara's heart. He sought not to dwell on the injustice bestowed upon him but instead focused on the path that lay before him—a path laden with opportunities for redemption and self-discovery.

"I stand ready to face the consequences of my supposed wrongdoings, even if it involves journeying through dangerous territories filled with fierce panthers," he confessed, a steeliness underlying his unwavering resolve. Vessantara's commitment to the path of righteousness and perfections, no matter the trials that lay in wait, emanated from the very core of his being.

With each word, he sought to assuage the concerns that undoubtedly welled within his mother's heart, assuring her of his unyielding dedication to goodness. "Even in the face of temptations that may beset me, I shall strive ceaselessly to uphold what is right," Vessantara promised, his voice carrying the weight of his unwavering integrity.

In that sad moment, the love and gratitude that swelled within Vessantara's eyes mirrored the profound bond between mother and son. Their connection transcended the realm of words, intertwining their spirits in a tapestry woven with unconditional love, strength, and resilience.

***

Queen Phusati appeared deeply saddened, with her face reflecting the weight of her sorrow. Her voice was shaky but graceful as she found the courage to speak. Tears streamed down her cheeks as she begged her son, the one she cherished so dearly.

"My dear son," she began, her voice laced with a bittersweet blend of love and resignation, "you are free to embark on this tough journey, and with my blessings, you shall depart. But leave behind your devoted wife, Maddi, and your cherished children. They cannot accompany you on this treacherous path." Her gaze fell upon Maddi, her daughter-in-law, her eyes tracing the delicate contours of her youthful beauty, a mirror of her own youth.

Her voice quivered with a mix of concern and pleading as she continued, her words carrying the weight of a mother's protective love. "Look at her, my dear son," Queen Phusati implored, her voice quivering with a delicate vulnerability. "See her fair and rounded limbs, her slender waist. Why must she be burdened with the trials that await you?" A shudder coursed through her, her sorrow finding the voice in the tears that streamed down her anguished face.

Queen Phusati's plea held within it a tapestry of emotions—love, anguish, and an unyielding desire to protect those she held dear. The corners of her heart were etched with the weight of motherly sacrifice, yet her soul yearned for the happiness and safety of her son and his beloved wife.

In that tender moment, the air seemed heavy with unspoken words and unfulfilled desires. The emotions that surged between mother and son transcended the limitations of mere language, a silent understanding that hung in the ethereal space between them.

"I shall never take a slave against her will," Vessantara proclaimed, his voice carrying the weight of his principles. His gaze swept across the faces of those assembled, his eyes gleaming with a deep-rooted empathy. "If she desires to accompany me on this journey, her heart yearning for the unknown path that lies ahead, then she shall be free to make that choice. But if her spirit finds solace in remaining here, surrounded by familiarity and the comforts she knows, then it is her right to stay."

In those transformative words, Vessantara revealed the true depths of his character and his unwavering commitment to justice and equality. The essence of his noble soul shone through, illuminating the room with a radiance that defied the confines of the physical realm. His understanding, born of profound empathy, extended beyond the boundaries of social hierarchy, recognizing the inherent worth and agency of those bound in servitude.

***

King Sanjaya's heart sank as he listened to his son's resolute words. He looked at Maddi with pleading eyes, his voice filled with desperation and longing.

"Dear Maddi, listen to me," the King implored, his voice trembling with emotion. "The life that awaits you in the forest is hardship and uncertainty. It is a life devoid of the comforts and luxuries you are accustomed to. Please, do not let the dust of the earth tarnish your lovely limbs. Do not exchange the exquisite garments of Benares for rough bark and coarse fabric. The forest is not a place fit for someone of your stature, my blessed Princess."

Maddi, adorned in her regal attire, met the King's gaze with unwavering determination. Her voice carried a steadfast resolve as she spoke, her words filled with love and devotion.

"I understand your concerns, dear father-in-law," she replied, her voice gentle yet firm. "But my happiness lies in the arms of my beloved Vessantara. I cannot forsake him, not even for the grandest of pleasures or the most opulent luxuries. The bond we share is stronger than any material comfort or societal expectation. Together, we will face the challenges of the forest and find joy in each other's presence. This is the path I have chosen, and I stand by it."

The mighty ruler of Sivi addressed Maddi once more, his tone filled with concern and caution. "Listen closely, dear Maddi, for I must share with you the dangers that await in the depths of the Himalayan forest. It is a land teeming with winged creatures, buzzing gnats, buzzing bees, and scuttling beetles, whose stings can inflict great harm and bring forth sickness."

"For those dwelling by the riverbanks, there is yet another menace that lurks. It is the boa constrictor, a formidable beast of immense strength whose bite may lack venom but whose grip is unyielding. Should any creature or soul cross its path, it will ensnare them in its powerful coils and drag them away to its hidden lair, a labyrinth of intertwined layers."

"But that is not all, Maddi, for the woods hold even more dangers. There, you shall encounter the fearsome bear, its coat a tangled mass of black fur, adept at scaling branches to ensnare its unsuspecting prey. And along the banks of Sotumbara, the arduous wild buffalo roams, its pointed horns capable of delivering a devastating blow."

"As you wander through the forest, you will witness vast herds of cows leisurely grazing, yet amidst their peaceful presence; you will feel a pang of distress akin to a lost cow searching for her young. And the trees, Maddi, they are inhabited by hordes of mischievous monkeys, a sight that may not bring you much pleasure."

"Even during the brightest hours of the day, when the birds rest, and the woods seem serene, you will find yourself surrounded by a cacophony of clamor, as if the very air itself resonates with the sounds of the wild. What is your plan now, dear Maddi, as you find yourself dwelling in the shadow of Vamka hill? Why would you choose to remain in such a place where every corner holds a potential threat?"

The King's words hung in the air, filled with genuine concern for Maddi's well-being. The weight of the forest's dangers pressed upon her, and she realized the magnitude of the decision before her.

Maddi listened carefully to the King's words, her eyes fixed on him as he spoke of the dangers that awaited her in the forest. The image of the boa constrictor coiling around its prey sent shivers down her spine, and the thought of being attacked by monkeys or bees made her anxious. But even with all these fears in her heart, she knew what she had to do.

With tearful eyes, Maddi turned to the King and spoke, her voice quivering with emotion, as she responded:
"To these frightening things you have told me,
I am prepared to heed,
No matter the obstacles and hardships that
I may need to lead.

With my own strength,
I'll make my way and never once concede.
A wife's duty is to keep her husband pleased,
She must perform her obligations without any ease.

Tending to the fire, cleaning spilled water,
rolling up dung, and more,
All for the sake of her husband's love,
to keep him by her side for sure.

But should she lose her husband,
a widow's fate is cruel and bleak,
Forced to make do with scraps, harassed,
and constantly weak.

No one dares to intervene
as she's trampled and pulled by her hair,

The misery of widowhood is too much to bear,
so, great King, I must go.

Yes, the desolation of widowhood is too much to take,
The sons of widows were treated with harsh blows,
as if they were a mistake.
Widowhood is a curse, a life that is wretched and low,
Great King, I must leave, for there's nowhere else to go.

No amount of silver and gold can erase the hurtful
words and taunts,
From family and acquaintances, a widow is the subject
of cruel taunts.
Alone in the midst of siblings, a widow's life is dreadful
and cold,
Great King, I must go, for my spirit is getting old.

A chariot is known by its banner, fire by its smoke,
A kingdom is recognized by its King, a bride by her
groom's cloak.
I'll stand by my husband, in wealth or in want,
For a wife who stays by her husband's side is praised by
even the gods, for she's valiant.

I'll put on his robes of yellow and be his Queen,
Together, we'll rule the land, a powerful and mighty team.
Widowhood is a dreadful thing, and I won't succumb to
its misery,
I will go, Your Majesty, to stand by my husband's side in
perfect harmony.
Those heartless women, devoid of compassion, are
incapable of empathy,

For when their husbands suffer, their only desire is personal healing.
If the King of Sivi is forced to leave and go into exile,
I'll go with him, for he's the bringer of joy and happiness."

***

King Sanjaya addressed Maddi, who was both bright and beautiful, and said, "Leave your two young children with us. They are too young to join you, but we will make sure to take care of them."

Maddi replied to the King in a voice that was both clear and fair:
"My Jali and Kanhajina are closest to my heart: They will come to the woods with me and together lighten my sorrow."

The King replied with great enthusiasm, expressing his concern for the children:
"Until now, they have been feasting on delicious cooked dishes,
If they must now rely on wild-tree fruits as their sustenance, what will become of the little ones?
From silver plates that had been adorned or those of gold,
The children ate: but what will they do if all that is left are leaves bare?
Benares cloth or linen was their clothing until now:
But what if they must wear grass or bark, what will the children do?
Previously, they had traveled in carriages or palanquins,
But when they are required to walk, what will the children do?

Until now, they had slept in secure, gabled rooms,
But when they are forced to take refuge beneath trees,
what will the children do?
Until now, they have been resting upon cushions, rugs,
or intricately crafted beds:
But what will the children do when they are laid out on
a bed of grass?
Previously, they were covered in delightful aromas and
fragrances:
What will the children do when they are smothered in
dirt and dust?
As the peacock's plumage and yak's tail fans have cooled
them thus far,
what can the children do when flies and insects attack
them?"

***

In the vibrant kingdom of Sivi, a tale unfolded, stirring
the hearts of its citizens and leaving an indelible mark
on their lives. The aged and the young, encompassing
every generation, stood united in a symphony of sorrow.
Tears cascaded down weathered cheeks, mingling with
the anguish that welled up from deep within their souls.
Their outstretched arms were a desperate plea, a
yearning to keep their beloved King, who had tended to
the kingdom of Sivi with unwavering care, within their
midst.

Among the grieving crowd, the courtiers and royal
consorts, adorned in resplendent garments, were not
exempt from the weight of sorrow that draped their
beings. They, too, joined the collective wail that resonated

through the corridors of the palace, lamenting the impending departure of Vessantara, who had nurtured their kingdom. The walls echoed their mournful cries as if in sympathy, amplifying the poignant atmosphere that pervaded the grand halls.

In the city that flourished under noble Vessantara's benevolent rule, the women, embodying the spirit and resilience of Sivi, wept unabatedly. They clung to the hope that their beseeching pleas would sway King Sanjaya's decision, for they were acutely aware of the immeasurable joy and security his presence had bestowed upon them. "It is a bad deed!" they exclaimed in despair, their voices trembling with an agonizing mix of grief and disbelief.

The young and old, without distinction, shared in the collective heartache that accompanied their beloved Prince's departure. The revered Brahmins and ascetics, who had found solace in Vessantara's generosity and kindness, were no exception. Their hearts shattered into fragments, for they had come to regard him as a guiding light, a beacon of wisdom in a world shrouded in darkness. Their lamentations merged with those of the townsfolk, forming a sorrowful chorus that carried far beyond the borders of Sivi.

As Vessantara made his somber preparations to leave, the weight of sorrow permeated the air. The town, once teeming with vibrancy, now found itself enveloped in a shroud of desolation. As they watched their beloved monarch depart, the people felt an unbearable weight in their hearts. They knew that their town would never be the same again, as the radiant presence that had once brought life to every corner was now gone forever.

And so, the fateful day drew to a close, leaving behind a trail of tears and grief in its wake. The people of Sivi wept and wailed, their hearts pierced by the painful reality of bidding farewell to their cherished Vessantara, for it was not a choice born of their own volition but a collective decision that had dictated his exile from the kingdom he had nurtured with boundless love.

***

Maddi looked into the eyes of her beloved husband, her voice gentle yet resolute, and said, "Worry not, my lord, and do not be perplexed today. Our journey may take us far and wide, but rest assured, wherever we may wander, our children shall not stray."

With those comforting words spoken, Maddi and her husband, Vessantara, set forth on their way, hand in hand, their children walking beside them with joyful anticipation.

As they journeyed, the people of Sivi lined the high road, bidding their beloved Vessantara and Maddi farewell. The air was filled with a mixture of emotions - sorrow, admiration, and a sense of reverence for the benevolent ruler they were about to lose.

But Vessantara remained true to his vow's decree, paying homage to his parents and showing love and loyalty to his people until the very end. He mounted the swift chariot, drawn by its team of four magnificent horses, and with his wife and children by his side, they ascended towards Vamka's peak.

The city streets were crowded with tearful faces, and as they passed through, Vessantara called out with a voice full of love and gratitude, "Farewell, dear kin, a blessed farewell! Though I must leave, my heart remains with you, and my love shall endure forever." The sound of his voice resonated through the streets, touching the hearts of all who heard it.

Amidst the gathered crowd, the Great Being, Vessantara, stood tall and radiant. His eyes glimmered with wisdom and compassion as he addressed his beloved people, advising them to remain vigilant and engage in acts of charity and kindness. The crowd listened intently, their hearts moved by his words, for they knew that their King was not just a ruler but a true embodiment of benevolence.

As the journey continued, Vessantara's mother, Queen Phusati, who understood her son's innate desire to give, sent two carts laden with precious ornaments and seven valuable treasures. Each cart moved gracefully, one on each side of Vessantara, symbolizing the boundless abundance of love and generosity within the royal family.

With a heart overflowing with generosity, Vessantara distributed all the gifts to the beggars and people in need he encountered along the road. He didn't hesitate to give away even the ornaments adorning his own body, for in his eyes, the joy of giving was far greater than any possession.

As the city slowly faded from view, Vessantara turned back to gaze upon it one last time. To his amazement, the earth seemed to respond to his wish, parting to accommodate the chariot's movement, allowing him to face the city and behold his parents' dwelling one more time. It was a divine occurrence, and it left those who witnessed it in awe of the greatness of their King.

Remarkable events followed in the wake of this divine occurrence, with the earth trembling like a grand banyan tree shaken by an unseen force and other wonders that could only be described as miraculous.

In the midst of these divine manifestations, Vessantara turned to his beloved wife Maddi, her eyes filled with wonder and love, and encouraged her to behold the place of beauty from which they had come - the majestic dwelling of King Sivi, their ancestral home.

With a regal demeanor, Vessantara turned his gaze towards the sixty thousand courtiers who had grown up alongside him, as well as the rest of the people who had gathered to witness the momentous occasion. His voice carried the weight of his noble purpose as he instructed them to return, his eyes filled with compassion and gratitude for their presence.

As the journey continued in the grand carriage, Vessantara turned to his beloved wife, Maddi, his eyes soft and full of love. He spoke to her in a gentle tone,

"My lady, keep a vigilant lookout to see if any suitors are following us." Ever dutiful, Maddi nodded, her eyes scanning their surroundings with unwavering attention.

Meanwhile, four Brahmins, who had missed the opportunity to witness the extraordinary distribution of the Seven Hundreds, had just arrived in the city. After learning that the generous giving had already concluded and Vessantara had departed, they asked anxiously, "Did he take anything with him?" The reply came, "Yes, he took a chariot." This led them to decide that they would approach Vessantara to request the horses.

As fate would have it, Maddi was quick to spot their approach. Her heart filled with compassion for these men in need, she softly exclaimed to the Great Being, "Beggars, my lord!" With profound wisdom and empathy, Vessantara halted the chariot, and the Brahmins approached with humble grace. They requested the horses, and without a moment's hesitation, Vessantara graciously granted their humble request.

At this moment, Vessantara's magnanimity shone brighter than ever. His heart knew no bounds, and his generosity touched the lives of people in need and those who witnessed this profound act of selflessness.

As the magnificent chariot continued its journey, Vessantara and his beloved Maddi immersed themselves in the enchanting forest's splendor. The woods seemed to come alive with mystical energy, and the air was imbued with an otherworldly aura. The moment the four Brahmins left with the horses, the yoke of the chariot defied gravity, remaining suspended in mid-air as if held by unseen hands.

However, the divine intervention did not end there. To the astonishment of everyone present, four majestic gods descended from the heavens, transforming themselves into resplendent red deer, their graceful forms glowing with celestial radiance. With effortless elegance, they stepped forward and took hold of the yoke as if they were benevolent spirits guiding the chariot on its path.

In awe of this miraculous sight, Vessantara turned to Maddi, his eyes shimmering with wonder and awe. In a hushed voice filled with reverence, he shared, "Behold, Maddi, an awe-inspiring sight, a true marvel to behold. These astute horses, transformed into red deer, guide us, as we're told!"

Maddi, too, was captivated by the divine spectacle before her. She felt a profound connection with the mystical realms that had graced their journey, as if the very essence of the universe embraced their purpose. Vessantara and Maddi exchanged a knowing glance, their souls intertwined by the shared wonder of this moment.

As the chariot journeyed further through the ethereal forest, another Brahmin, deeply moved by the divine presence he had just witnessed, appeared before the Great Being. With humility and respect, he made a humble request for the chariot, recognizing the virtue and kindness that radiated from Vessantara.

Illustration 3: Accompanied by his wife and children, Vessantara embarks on a journey into the forest for exile. Along the way, they encounter Brahmins who request their horses and chariot.

Understanding the significance of this moment and the impact of his actions on the lives of others, Vessantara gracefully descended from the majestic carriage. He stood before the petitioner with a warm smile and an open heart, ready to bestow the chariot with unparalleled generosity. He was a living testament to the power of selfless giving and the boundless love he held for his fellow beings.

As Vessantara granted the chariot to the new petitioner, an aura of sacredness surrounded the moment. It was as if the gods were witnessing this profound act of compassion, their divine presence illuminating the forest with ethereal light. And with the fulfillment of this benevolent act, the gods in the form of red deer, having served their divine purpose, vanished from sight, leaving behind a trail of blessings and divine grace.

***

Once the majestic chariot had been bestowed upon the grateful Brahmin, the Great Being, Vessantara, and Maddi embarked on the next leg of their journey on foot. As they ventured into the heart of the mystical forest, the atmosphere was imbued with a sense of divine presence, and every step they took seemed to echo with ancient wisdom.

Drawing Maddi close, Vessantara gently spoke with unwavering love and concern, "Maddi, take Kanhajina, for she is young and light, and I shall carry Jali with all my strength. Let us continue this path together, my dear, for the road ahead may be challenging, but we shall endure as one."

With their children cradled tenderly in their arms, the royal couple embarked on their journey, their spirits undeterred by the trials that lay ahead. Whenever they encountered fellow travelers along the road, they diligently inquired about the route to Vamaka Hill, their destination of hope and promise.

CHAPTER 4

JOURNEY THROUGH THE DEEP
FOREST

With warm hearts, the kind-hearted strangers shared their wisdom and guidance, revealing that their path was long and arduous. Yet, despite the warning of challenging terrains and treacherous paths, the Great Being Vessantara and Maddi remained steadfast and unwavering. They were driven by an uncompromising commitment to their divine purpose, guided by the virtues of compassion and selflessness that defined their very souls.

They met many sympathetic travelers throughout their journey, each offering a tearful gaze of understanding. Each encounter reinforced the enormity of their sacrifice and the profound impact of their love for the people they had served. The tears they shared were not of regret or sorrow but a testament to the depth of their devotion and the boundless spirit of generosity that defined their being.

The dense forest enveloped them with an enchanting ambiance as the royal family continued their journey along the winding road. The lush canopy above, adorned with various fruits, ignited the children's hearts with wonder and excitement. Kanhajina and Jali gazed in awe at the colorful fruits hanging tantalizingly from the branches on both sides of the path. Their eyes sparkled with innocent curiosity, and their hearts fluttered with longing to taste the succulent offerings of nature.

Overwhelmed by their desire, tears welled up in their innocent eyes, expressing their longing for the sweet delights just out of their reach. Their yearning touched the depths of Maddi's heart, witnessing the children's innocent desires and aspirations. Gently, she wiped away their tears, consoling them with a tender smile.

Moved by the children's heartfelt longing, the Great Being, Vessantara, felt a surge of compassion surging through him. With a touch of his extraordinary power, he caused the very trees to respond to the children's innocent wishes. As if answering a silent plea, the trees gracefully bent down, lowering their laden branches within the children's reach.

Elated, Kanhajina and Jali reached out, plucking the ripest fruits with sheer delight. The forest seemed to dance with joy as the children's laughter echoed through its verdant halls. Each fruit they picked felt like a treasured gift, lovingly bestowed upon them by the benevolent trees themselves.

***

Amazement filled Maddi's heart as she beheld the extraordinary sight unfolding before her. The Great Being, her beloved husband, stood at the edge of the cliff, his presence commanding the attention of all who witnessed it. His power, a testament to his boundless love and compassion, touched the very essence of her soul.

"This is truly a marvel!" she exclaimed, her voice brimming with awe and admiration. Her radiant expression mirrored the ethereal beauty of the moment, and in that instant, she found herself overwhelmed by the greatness of her husband—the one who had healed her wounds, whispered courage in her darkest hours, and held her heart with unwavering devotion.

The moment weaves together love, wonder, and the exceptional depth of their bond.

***

From the grand city of Jetuttara, nestled amidst lush landscapes and bustling with life, the magnificent mountain named Suvannagiritala stood tall, adorned with golden hues, a sight to behold, and a journey of five leagues away. From there, the gentle flow of the river Kontimara whispered its tales of the land, inviting travelers to its banks, beckoning them with its refreshing embrace, another five leagues away. Beyond the river's embrace, Mount Aranjaragiri rose majestically, its peaks brushing the heavens, another five leagues to traverse.

Undeterred by the distance, the noble family embarked on their odyssey, each step bringing them closer to their destination. The next leg of their journey led them to the Brahmin village of Dunnivittha, where warm hospitality and spiritual wisdom intertwined, yet another five leagues away. With unwavering resolve and the spirit of adventure guiding their path, they pressed on, moving gracefully through the vast lands, bridging the gap between cities, hearts intertwined with hope and love.

As the sun cast its radiant glow upon the horizon, bathing the world in hues of orange and gold, they continued their journey, traversing another ten leagues, each step leading them closer to their uncle's city. The Great Being's thoughts wandered to his dear uncle, the wise and venerable ruler of the kingdom they sought, eager to reunite with family and share the story of their noble journey.

Yet, the Yakkhas themselves took notice of the family's quest, their hearts moved by the innocence and purity of Kanhajina and Jali. In their benevolence, they decided to bestow a divine gift upon the noble family, shortening the distance of their journey. Time seemed to fold, and the expanse between cities diminished, all in the name of compassion and understanding.

The journey that would have taken several days now materialized before their eyes within a single day's passage. The gods' intervention allowed the Great Being Vessantara and his beloved family to reach the kingdom of Ceta and his uncle's city before the veil of twilight adorned the skies.

Amidst the vibrant colors of the setting sun, they stepped into the kingdom, welcomed by the embrace of love and joy. The saying echoed through the hearts of the people, narrating the tale of divine intervention and compassion:

"The Yakkhas made the journey short, pitying the children's plight,

And so, to Ceta kingdom, they arrived before the night."

Their incredible journey was a testament to the unbreakable bonds of love and the blessings of divine guardians. It became etched into the annals of legend, a tale that would be recounted for generations to come. The noble family's resilience, the kindness of the gods, and their spirit of giving came together to create a magnificent tapestry of compassion and wonder.

As the sun dipped below the horizon, the city of Ceta embraced its prodigal son, the Great Being, and his family. Warm embraces and joyous laughter welcomed them, reuniting hearts long separated by distance and circumstance.

Thus, from the city of Jetuttara, their journey spanned thirty leagues, a distance they had triumphed over with unwavering love and devotion. The gods had smiled upon them, shortening the distance with their divine touch, a testament to the enduring power of compassion.

***

In the heart of his uncle's city, the Great Being Vessantara found himself amidst a realm of sixty thousand Khattiyas, their presence as vast and impressive as the city itself. The bustling streets beckoned, but the noble soul chose to pause, electing to take refuge in a hall located right at the grand gates of the city. With a tender touch, Maddi cared for his feet, the very feet that had carried him on an extraordinary journey of generosity and selflessness.

As Maddi stepped out of the hall to position herself within sight, word of their arrival quickly spread. Her elegance and grace caught the eyes of the passersby, drawing them like moths to a flame. Mesmerized, they gathered around her, curious about the noble lady whose heart was so closely entwined with that of the Great Being.

The gathering of a multitude of people created a low murmur that filled the air. The sight that lay before them stirred something deep within their hearts. Vessantara, an epitome of kindness, stood beside Maddi, both embracing their children, a living embodiment of their love and commitment. In the presence of this exceptional family, emotions ran high, and the people of the city were profoundly moved, their spirits lifted by the unwavering love and devotion on display.

***

News of their arrival swiftly reached the ears of the King, who was none other than the uncle of Vessantara himself. Overwhelmed with grief and sorrow, sixty thousand princes, cousins of the noble soul, wept and lamented as they made their way towards the King's court. The heart of the city resonated with their mournful cries.

As the princes stood before their King, they pleaded for his understanding and compassion. Amid their sorrow, the Great Being, Vessantara addressed them with a voice of calm and wisdom, sharing the tale of his extraordinary journey and the reason behind his arrival.

With sincerity and humility, he expressed his gratitude for their concern, assuring them of his well-being and prosperity. He spoke of his heartfelt gift to his father, a savior elephant with unmatched power and grandeur, adorned with jewels and fit for a King to ride. However, fate had taken an unexpected turn, for his father perceived the gift as a cause for discord and strife. Thus, he had been banished, and now, he sought a new life, a place where he and his family could thrive, away from the palace walls.

Seeking the guidance of his esteemed cousins, Vessantara conveyed his wish for a place to call his own, a dwelling where the echoes of compassion and love would reverberate through its halls, a sanctuary far from the kingdom he once knew.

***

The princes, with hearts full of compassion and determination, listened intently to Vessantara's words. Their eyes, gleaming with respect for the noble King before them, bore witness to the depth of their admiration. They understood the weight of his words and the burden of his banishment, and their commitment to support him grew even stronger.

"Hail, O mighty King," they replied, their voices resonating with unwavering conviction. "You need not worry, for in our realm, you shall be the master of all, free to make your own choices. These herbs, roots, honey, meat, and rice we offer are the finest and the best, a symbol of our gratitude and esteem. Enjoy them at your pleasure, O King, and be our esteemed guest."

Vessantara's gratitude was evident in his gaze as he thanked them for their generous gifts and kind intentions. But his mind was set on his journey, guided by the decree of his banishment from the kingdom of Sivi. "Your hospitality warms my heart, noble princes," he spoke with unwavering resolve. "But as you know, King Sanjaya has banished me, and to Vamka hill, I must venture. I seek your guidance, dear cousins, for a dwelling to call my own, a place where I may reside as I embrace this new journey alone."

The princes, caring deeply for their cousin, were quick to offer their support. "Stay here in Ceta, O mighty King," they suggested, their voices filled with hope. "While we send word to the King of Sivi land, informing him of the truth and reason behind your journey. Surely, once he knows, he shall understand."

United in purpose, they formed a joyous procession, ready to stand by Vessantara in this pivotal moment.

They believed in the power of truth and the righteousness of their cause, confident that their words would sway the heart of the King of Sivi.

But the Great Being, wise beyond measure, intervened with a word of caution. "I must advise you against sending word to the King," he spoke with solemnity. "For his reign has been cast into doubt, and the palace and townsfolk are engulfed in discontent. They seek to challenge him for my banishment, and such turmoil could lead to an ill fate for all."

The princes considered the dire possibility, realizing the implications of their actions. "If such unrest engulfs the kingdom," they pondered, "then we shall abide by your wishes, O revered King. Stay with us, assume your regal state here in Ceta, and let your reign be one of prosperity and unity."

Yet, Vessantara's heart remained steadfast in his decision. "Your offer is deeply appreciated, sons of Ceta," he spoke with gratitude. "But as an exiled man, I cannot accept this throne and sway. The people of Sivi would be displeased, and strife and discord may follow. I must avoid such outcomes, and so I humbly request your guidance in finding a dwelling where I may reside as I continue this journey, guided by the path of my banishment."

His words, spoken with modesty and determination, touched the hearts of the princes. They respected his resolve and understood the importance of his quest. With a shared sense of purpose, they vowed to support him in finding a suitable abode, a sanctuary where he could find solace amidst the trials of banishment.

And so, guided by compassion and determination, the princes led their revered cousin on a search for the perfect dwelling, a place that would become his refuge in the face of adversity.

***

Despite numerous requests and great honor from the princes, the Great Being firmly declined the offer of the kingdom. Instead, he chose to remain in the hall just outside the city walls. Touched by the Princess' kindness, he gratefully accepted their gesture of adorning the hall and surrounding it with a screen, providing him with comfort and security during his stay. The vigilant princes took every measure to ensure his comfort and safety, preparing a grand bed and keeping a watchful eye on the hall, both day and night.

As the first light of dawn brushed the horizon, Vessantara emerged from the hall, accompanied by the princes. They set forth together, walking side by side for fifteen leagues, surrounded by a substantial group of sixty thousand Khattiyas. With each step, the bond between them grew stronger, and the air hummed with a mix of solemnity and fondness.

As they reached the entrance of the dense wood, the Princess shared valuable guidance for the remaining fifteen leagues of the Great Being's journey. Each word carried a deep sense of purpose and care for their departing King.

"Towards the north lies the majestic mountain Gandhamadana," they began, their voices filled with reverence. "A place of serene beauty, where you and your family may find solace and nirvana. Further north, you'll encounter Mount Vipula, a delightful sight, with abundant trees and soothing shades, offering respite from the world's cares."

Flowing gracefully from the hill, they described Ketumati, a deep river adorned with fish-filled waters, a blessing for travelers seeking refreshment. "Rest, drink, bathe, and play with your children by its serene shore," they continued, "Find comfort beneath the banyan tree, laden with fruits galore."

Their words were like a map, guiding the Great Being's path through the wilderness. "Proceeding onward, you'll come across Mount Nalika, a place steeped in tales of enchantment," they narrated. "Songful birds and woodland sprites create a harmonious symphony around. Towards the north lies Mucalinda Lake, a scenic place, covered in lilies, offering solace and tranquility."

With each description, the Great Being's heart felt lighter, knowing that his journey would be adorned with such natural wonders. "Through the lush and green forest, like a cloud overhead," they spoke, "Venture, like a lion in search of prey to be fed. In the flowering woods, melodies of birds will fill the air, Their joyous twittering, a harmonious affair."

As they shared tales of beauty and enchantment, they also provided practical wisdom. "Follow the mountain cataracts to their source," they advised, "and discover a lily-covered lake with blossoms overhead. Plentiful fish and tranquility will abound, and there, build a leafy cell, a hermitage profound."

The Great Being nodded in deep appreciation, absorbing their words like precious gems. "From your cell," they continued, "venture for sustenance and return with grace; embrace this serene journey as you seek enlightenment's embrace."

With these directions imprinted in his mind and heart, the Great Being was allowed to proceed on his path. The wise and skilled princes ensured that his safety was well-guarded, leaving no room for adversaries to interfere.

And so, with a heart filled with gratitude, love, and resolve, the Great Being Vessantara bid farewell to the princes, thanking them for their unwavering support and care. Silently vowing to uphold the virtues that had brought them together, Vessantara watched them disappear into the horizon. They returned to their city, their minds and souls enriched by the presence of such a noble soul, their King, embarking on a journey that would test his resilience, compassion, and understanding of the human experience. As they parted ways, the spirit of unity and kinship lingered, forever etched in the tapestry of their shared destinies.

***

Illustration 4: Prince Vessantara, accompanied by his wife Princess Maddi and their two children, enters exile in the forest.

As the sun gently embraced the horizon, painting the sky with hues of gold and pink, Prince Vessantara, accompanied by his beloved wife Maddi and their two cherished children, continued their journey towards the wondrous realm of Gandhamadana. Their path meandered through landscapes both enchanting and untamed, each step drawing them closer to the heart of nature's embrace.

Upon arriving at Mount Gandhamadana, they found themselves amidst a panorama of unparalleled beauty. The air was scented with the fragrance of blossoms, and the earth seemed to pulse with the rhythm of life. Here, time seemed to flow at a different pace, and Vessantara and his family felt a profound sense of serenity enveloping their hearts. They chose to rest for a day, savoring the tranquility that the sacred place offered.

As the morning sun gently touched the horizon, they turned their sights northward, embarking on the next leg of their journey. The landscape began to change, and they soon found themselves passing by the foot of the majestic Mount Vipula. The sight of the mountain's peaks reaching for the heavens filled them with awe and wonder, reminding them of the world's vastness and their own souls.

Continuing their way, they found themselves drawn to the tranquil bank of the river Ketumati, a place of serenity where a generous forester welcomed them with open arms. Overwhelmed by the warmth of their reception, the Great Being and his family partook in a delectable meal, their hearts filled with gratitude for the kindness bestowed upon them. As a token of their appreciation, they offered the forester a golden hairpin, a symbol of their gratitude and a reflection of their noble character.

They resumed their journey with renewed vigor, crossing the stream with grace and composure. Seeking refuge beneath a grand banyan tree that grew on a flat expanse of the mountain, they found solace in the shade it provided. The banyan tree bore fruits of divine sweetness, and the family savored the bounty it offered, cherishing each moment of unity and love shared under its ancient branches.

Their path continued to unfold before them, leading them towards the Nalika hill. As they pressed forward, they traced the gentle curves of Lake Mucalinda, its tranquil waters reflecting the endless sky. Arriving at its northeastern corner, they embraced the peaceful energy that emanated from the lake, feeling at one with nature's grand design.

Undeterred by the wilderness that lay ahead, they ventured deeper into the dense forest, following a narrow footpath. The sounds of the forest seemed to whisper secrets of the ancients, and the air hummed with a sense of mystique and wonder. A gentle stream, born from the mountain's heart, guided them onward, its babbling waters a soothing companion on their journey.

Finally, they reached their destination, a peaceful and foursquare lake nestled like a precious gem amidst the embrace of the forest. The lake exuded an aura of wisdom, inviting them to ponder the mysteries of existence. The Great Being and his family found a sanctuary for their souls amid untamed nature, a space where their spirits could find solace and renewal.

***

In the ethereal realm of the gods, Sakka, the mighty King of divine beings, gazed upon the unfolding events with keen interest. His eyes, ablaze with celestial wisdom, observed the Great Being, Vessantara, as he crossed the threshold into the sacred realm of Himavat, seeking solace and a dwelling for his noble family. With a sense of compassion, Sakka realized the noble intentions of the exiled King and recognized the importance of his journey.

Moved by the Great Being Vessantara's quest, Sakka summoned Vissakamma, the celestial architect known for his unparalleled skill and craftsmanship. The divine realm buzzed with anticipation as King Sakka entrusted Vissakamma with a sacred mission: to create a haven of tranquility and beauty upon the enchanting valleys of Mount Vamka, where the Great Being Vessantara and his cherished family could find shelter and peace.

Vissakamma embraced the task with enthusiasm and devotion. With the touch of his divine hands, he molded two hermitages, each a testament to celestial artistry. Covered walks, gracefully adorned with carvings of heavenly beings, meandered through the tranquil landscape. The day and night rooms stood tall, welcoming the weary travelers to find respite within their comforting embrace. In the verdant surroundings, rows of flowering trees, their petals awash with the colors of dawn, and clusters of banana plants swayed in harmony, creating an idyllic setting for the seekers of solitude.

To announce the hermitages' purpose to those searching for a higher calling, Vissakamma inscribed a welcome message upon the walls, written with golden letters: "These are meant for those aspiring to be hermits." As if woven by celestial hands, the script glowed with an otherworldly luminescence, guiding them toward their sanctuary of contemplation.

With meticulous attention to detail, Vissakamma ensured the serenity of the hermitages. Any inhuman creatures or noisy beasts and birds were gently escorted away, allowing the air to be filled with nothing but the soothing symphony of nature's whispers.

The divine architect's masterpiece was completed, and he cast a final glance upon the hermitages, marveling at the beauty that had taken shape under his hands. With a sense of profound satisfaction, he bid farewell to the enchanting haven, his heart rejoicing at the thought of the peace and solace it would offer its future inhabitants.

Upon his return to the celestial abode, Sakka, too, felt content, knowing that he had played a part in supporting the noble journey of the Great Being. He looked down upon the hermitages from his celestial throne, their roofs shimmering with stardust, and sent his blessings upon the tranquil abode.

***

In the vast expanse of Mount Vamka's enchanting valleys, the Great Being, Vessantara, and his beloved family found themselves amidst a haven of tranquility and spiritual solace. The hermitages were crafted with great care by the divine architect Vissakamma, and they were a true testament to celestial beauty and divine craftsmanship. The walls of the hermitages were adorned with intricate carvings of heavenly beings, which seemed to whisper tales of ancient wisdom and enlightenment to those who sought refuge in them.

Upon discovering a hidden path that seemed to signal him, Vessantara's heart stirred with a profound intuition that it would lead to the very hermitage meant for his family. With a gentle kiss upon Maddi's forehead, he reassured her and the two children, Kanhajina and Jali, as he ventured into the verdant embrace of the forest. A hushed serenity enveloped the surroundings as he made his way toward the heart of the sacred realm.

And there it stood before him, a hermitage of divine grace and spiritual wisdom. The inscription, gleaming with ethereal light, bore witness to the celestial knowledge that Sakka, the King of gods, had been aware of his presence and had prepared this sanctuary for him. A deep sense of reverence filled Vessantara's soul as he removed his princely garb, setting aside his bow and sword, and donned the humble attire of a hermit. Taking up a staff, he embraced the symbol of his new way of life, a life dedicated to spiritual contemplation and selflessness.

With serene steps, he paced the covered walk, his heart resonating with the wisdom of the ages. As he approached the entrance where Maddi and the children stood, their eyes met, and an unspoken understanding passed between them. At that moment, Vessantara's aura seemed to mirror that of a Pacceka Buddha, radiating a profound sense of peace and wisdom.

Tears glistened in Maddi's eyes as she fell to her knees before her noble husband, overwhelmed by the beauty of his transformation. She knew that they were now embarking on a sacred path guided by the divine hand of Sakka. Filled with awe and reverence, she, too, shed her princely attire, embracing the simplicity of the ascetic dress, and entered her own cell adjacent to Vessantara's.

The two children, young and impressionable, followed the example set by their parents, embracing the new way of life with innocent curiosity and reverence. As they adorned the humble robes of hermits, their little hearts seemed to dance with the joy of discovery.

With the hermitage as their sanctuary, the four noble souls embraced their secluded realm of solitude, dedicating their days to spiritual contemplation and inner growth. Their days were adorned with simplicity and divine presence, the whispers of nature guiding their journey.

Maddi, now settled in her ascetic role, felt a deep sense of purpose in caring for her family and providing sustenance for all three. With a tender smile, she made a request to Vessantara, "My lord, allow me to venture into the forest and gather wild fruits for us, and I shall also care for our beloved children." Vessantara, deeply appreciative of her unwavering devotion, granted her request with a gentle nod.

However, seeking to safeguard the purity of their spiritual journey, Vessantara approached Maddi with a heartfelt plea. "My beloved, as we embark on this sacred path, and temptation can cloud even the purest intentions; I implore you to refrain from approaching me inappropriately. Let our bond be one of spiritual communion and transcendence."

Maddi's eyes shone with love and understanding as she tenderly cupped his face, assuring him, "My lord, you need not worry. I shall honor your request and tread this path with reverence and unwavering devotion."

The boundless compassion of Vessantara extended its gentle touch even to the creatures inhabiting the woods surrounding their dwelling. A beautiful and tranquil transformation began to unfold as harmony replaced hostility among these once-wild beings. As the first light of day painted the sky each morning, Maddi stirred from her slumber. With a heart brimming with kindness, she embarked on her daily ritual of tending to the animals that had become their unspoken companions.

Once wary and distant, the wild creatures now approached with trust and expectancy as Maddi provided them with water and sustenance. Her hands moved with grace, a symphony of gestures conveying love and care. Her children, nestled under the protective wing of their father, followed her example, learning the art of compassion from their mother's tender actions. Teeth were cleaned with the gentleness only a mother's touch could bring, and the space they called home was swept and tidied, a reflection of the serenity they nurtured within.

With her children under the watchful gaze of the Great Being, Maddi ventured into the verdant embrace of the forest. The tools of her task, a sturdy basket, a shovel, and a hook, accompanied her as she sought the wild treasures that nature so generously offered. Amidst the rustling leaves and dappled sunlight, she gathered roots and fruits, her fingers moving with practiced ease. Every piece of sustenance collected was a testament to the harmony that now danced between humankind and the wild.

***

As the golden sun dipped below the horizon, its last rays painted the landscape in hues of amber and rose. Maddi returned, her basket brimming with the abundance of the forest. The nourishment was carefully placed within their humble abode, a haven of simplicity and tranquility. With tender hands, she washed her children, cleansing the day's adventures from their innocent faces.

The arrival of the evening meal marked a cherished moment of togetherness. Their family of three gathered outside, the cool mountain breeze carrying with it a sense of unity and contentment. Fruits were savored not only for their taste but for the shared moments they represented. Laughter and conversation flowed freely, painting the air with a tapestry of love and belonging.

As the meal concluded, the Great Being's blessings were palpable in the air, a whispered reminder of the serenity they had cultivated. With a sense of quiet satisfaction, Maddi guided her children to their own abodes, a tender goodnight exchanged before they retired for rest.

And so, for seven months, they carved out a life on the mountain, each day a testament to the transformative power of kindness and compassion. The once-wild animals had become friends, the forest a supplier of sustenance, and their hearts a sanctuary of love.

CHAPTER 5

ENCOUNTER WITH BRAHMIN JUJAKA

During that period, in the Kingdom of Kalinga, a Brahmin named Jujaka lived in a village called Dunnivittha. Through humble alms-seeking, he managed to gather a hundred rupees, a small fortune in those times. Entrusting this sum to a fellow Brahmin family, he embarked on a quest to accumulate further wealth, hoping to augment his modest fortune. Yet, as fate would have it, his journey extended far beyond what he initially anticipated, and during his absence, the family he trusted had to use the money for their own needs.

Upon his eventual return, Jujaka was met with the harsh reality that the funds were gone, resulting from dire circumstances rather than any ill intentions. Bitterness mingled with frustration as he confronted the family.

But faced with their inability to repay the sum, they offered an alternative solution—a gesture of reparation. The Brahmin's eyes met those of a young maiden, Amittatapana, whom they provided as compensation.

Accepting their proposition, the Brahmin took Amittatapana under his care, bringing her with him as he returned to his home in Dunnivittha. In this humble village, the young woman shouldered the responsibility of looking after the aging Brahmin. Her diligence in this task was a beacon of devotion, illuminating the stark contrast between her care and the perceived neglect of the young Brahmin wives. The village's whispers held stories of Amittatapana's tireless dedication, and they carried with them a certain reproach for those who failed to emulate her.

As word spread of Amittatapana's exceptional qualities, whispers of admiration and comparison began to circulate among the young Brahmin wives in the village. However, these murmurs soon reached the ears of those who were the subjects of this unspoken critique, and jealousy began to take root in their hearts like an approaching storm cloud. Driven by feelings of insecurity and resentment, these women, united in their intentions, began to plot Amittatapana's removal from the village.

In groups, they assembled by the riverside and other communal spaces. Heavy with spite, their words were launched like arrows at Amittatapana, her heart the target of their cruelty. The virtues that made her a model of compassion were now the sources of their venomous words. Amidst their gatherings, the air became thick with the toxicity of their resentment, leaving no doubt about their collective intentions.

Down by the riverbank, where women gathered with their water pots, a chorus of critical whispers swirled around Amittatapana. This young woman, graced with youth and beauty, found herself at the center of their disapproving conversations. To these villagers, it was an affront to common sense that such a youthful soul should be bound to an aged man.

Their hushed voices dripped with judgment as they condemned what they perceived as a cruel twist of fate. In their minds, a web of deceit spun by Amittatapana's parents had trapped her in this unfortunate alliance with an older man. The village women united in their assumptions, painted a grim picture of the young woman's life, imagining her existence overshadowed by a union with a man of such advanced years.

Their empathy turned to sorrow as they discussed Amittatapana's hardships—her days marked by the burden of an aged companion. They spoke as if her youth had been stolen, leaving her with a heavy heart and the constant presence of a man who was much older than her. They were so convinced of this that they even considered that death might have been a more merciful fate for her.

Their judgment was not limited to Amittatapana alone; her parents faced their share of reproach. These women painted a vivid image of a heartless scheme devised by her parents, a plan that seemingly left no room for the aspirations and desires of their own daughter. They questioned the kindness of these parents who, in their eyes, had not secured a more suitable match for their daughter.

In the midst of a heated discussion, the topic of religious rituals and past offerings came up. The women, united by their shared disapproval, began to question the effectiveness of Amittatapana's prior devotion. They went as far as to suggest that the gods themselves might not look favorably upon a union that appeared to go against the natural order of things. The conversation was tense, and the air was thick with uncertainty as everyone waited to see how things would unfold.

The metaphor of pain and harm was invoked to underscore their perspective further. Being with an aged husband, they argued, was akin to being wounded by a sharp spear or bitten by a venomous snake. In their eyes, the older man brought not the warmth of companionship nor the delight of pleasant conversations; even his laughter was tainted by his age.

With conviction, they shared their belief that youthful company had the power to heal the aches of the heart. Their sentiment was clear: Amittatapana, vibrant and beautiful, deserved a partner who could match her in youthful spirit and bring happiness to her days.

Wrapped in their words was a kernel of advice, however sternly put. They advised Amittatapana to turn back, to return to the comfort of her home, for a life intertwined with an older man could only promise a barren field devoid of joy and delight.

***

When the backbiting women's laughter stung her heart, Amittatapana retreated to the shelter of her home, her water pot clutched in one hand and tears flowing down her cheeks. At the doorway, her husband, Jujaka, noticed her distress and his brows furrowed with concern.

"Why do tears stain your cheeks, my dear?" Jujaka's voice was gentle, laced with worry.

Amittatapana struggled to compose herself, her voice quivering as she responded, "I cannot bear their mocking words any longer. They ridicule me for being wed to a man of advanced years, and their scorn makes my heart ache."

Jujaka's features hardened as he listened, his protective instincts flaring. "You need not subject yourself to their taunts, my love. I shall fetch the water myself. Their words need not wound you any further."

Tears glistened in Amittatapana's eyes as she shook her head. "No, fetching water is not solely the issue. Our way of life and our roles are being twisted. I cannot bear it. Unless we have a servant to share the burden, I shall not stay."

Jujaka's brow furrowed, and he spoke earnestly, "But where would I find a servant, my dear? Our coffers lack the coin to secure such aid. Please, do not be angry. I will do my best to manage."

Illustration 5: Jujaka and his beautiful young wife, Amittapana.

Amittatapana's eyes held a determined gleam. "Listen to me, my husband. There is a solution. It is said that Prince Vessantara, a benevolent man, resides on Vamka hill. Go to him and request a servant to ease our toil. I believe he will grant our plea."

A sigh escaped Jujaka's lips, and he looked weary. "You see, my love, the journey is long, the path rugged, and my age frail. But worry not; I shall strive to fulfill your wishes."

Amittatapana's gaze remained resolute. "Do not surrender before you even begin, dear husband. Remember, you are a soldier facing the battle of life. Unless a servant is secured, mark my words, I shall leave. Our paths will diverge, and my happiness will be found in another's embrace."

Jujaka's eyes reflected both understanding and determination. "Fear not, my love, my dear, I shall prove my unwavering commitment. Even with my age's weight, I shall shoulder this responsibility."

Amittatapana's voice held a finality, "Remember, I have warned you. Our fates are intertwined with this decision, and I shall not waver."

The atmosphere settled heavily between them as Jujaka prepared himself for the journey. With a sense of trepidation and love, he spoke to his wife once more, his voice laden with emotion.

"Before I depart, gather provisions for my travels, my dear. Prepare a honey cake, bannocks, and barley bread, and two sturdy slaves shall accompany me. They shall serve us diligently, alleviating our burdens in your absence."

***

Amittatapana, ever devoted, swiftly arranged the provisions as requested, assuring him that all was ready. While she prepared, he attended to fortifying their dwelling, strengthening its weak spots, and securing the door to safeguard her during his absence. He gathered wood from the forest, ensuring their hearth would remain warm, and fetched water, filling every pitcher, pot, and pan for her convenience.

With a resolve akin to an ascetic's, he donned the humble garb of a seeker, and with words of caution and care, he bid his wife farewell. "Do not venture out at inopportune moments, and take every precaution until my return," he advised her.

Having taken his leave, he circled his beloved wife rightward, following the sacred custom, and began his journey with tearful eyes, emotions welling up inside him. His path led him toward the grand and opulent Sivi capital, where destiny awaited him, in search of a slave as requested by his wife Amittatapana.

His footsteps marked the path of sacrifice and devotion, a husband's unwavering love for his wife, and a commitment to fulfill her wish. In the vibrant realm of Sivi, a fateful encounter awaited the Brahmin, one that would ripple through the tapestry of their lives, entwining with the tale of the Great Being, who embarked on a journey of compassion and self-discovery. Like an invisible thread, destiny connected their lives in unforeseen ways as they tread the paths laid before them with courage and hope.

***

In the bustling city, the Brahmin found himself surrounded by a curious and helpful crowd. Eager to fulfill his wife's wishes, he urgently inquired, "Where can I find Vessantara? Where does the Prince reside now?" The people, in unison, responded with clarity, their voices carrying the tale of Prince Vessantara's boundless generosity, "By giving, giving endlessly, he was banished from this land. With his wife and kin, he now dwells in Vamka hill, where a new chapter of his life unfolds."

The Brahmin, burdened by remorse for his past actions, now faced the consequences of his insatiable greed. He found himself alone in the wilderness, where beasts and panthers roamed freely. Armed with his staff, begging bowl, and sacrificial spoon, he set forth into the unknown forest, seeking the one who bestowed blessings upon all.

As he navigated through the dense woods, he encountered the haunting howls of wolves, disrupting his path and leading him astray. Frustrated and disoriented, the Brahmin voiced his despair to the uncaring wilderness, "Who will tell me of Vessantara, the great and mighty King? The giver of peace in times of fear, to whom all suitors bring their pleas. They journey like rivers to the sea, seeking his endless favors to receive. Who will guide me to Vessantara, so great, kind, and brave?"

In his heart, he saw Vessantara as a serene lake adorned with lilies, offering refuge to all living souls, a place where hearts find restoration. He compared the King to a fig tree on a weary road, providing much-needed rest, or a banyan, sal, or mango tree, offering shelter to the oppressed.

Desperate for guidance in the vast and unforgiving forest, the Brahmin longed for a sympathetic ear, "Who will lend an ear to my troubled plea in this vast forest domain? A great blessing it would be to find the King so free."

His earnest call for assistance resonated in the wilderness, hoping to find the kind and benevolent Vessantara amidst the trees, rivers, and wilderness. A journey of redemption and discovery awaited the Brahmin as he sought the help of the Great Being.

***

Deep in the heart of the woods, the man assigned to watch over the kingdom's boundaries heard the Brahmin's desperate and lamenting cries. Suspicion immediately clouded his mind as he wondered about the stranger's true intentions. With a firm determination to protect Vessantara, Maddi, and their children, he resolved to confront the intruder, bow in hand, prepared to defend their sanctuary.

"You, Brahmin! Your presence here arouses suspicion," the forester declared, his voice tinged with caution and hostility. "Are you here to bring harm upon great King Vessantara, his family, or the peaceful inhabitants of this land?" He glared at the Brahmin, ready to act swiftly to safeguard their secluded dwelling.

The Brahmin, taken aback by the forester's aggressive stance, hurriedly explained, "Noble forester, I assure you, my intentions are pure and virtuous. I seek no harm but rather come seeking Vessantara's dwelling with reverence and respect." He paused, carefully choosing his words to allay the man's fears.

With conviction, Jujaka continued, "The great King faced the bitter fate of exile due to his unwavering dedication to giving endlessly. Now, he resides in the serene Vamka hill, embracing his new way of life. I, too, acknowledge the folly of my wanderings, like a lost crane chasing an elusive fish. But fear not, for I come in peace, seeking only to find the trace of the noble King Vessantara."

Yet, the forester remained resolute, the tension palpable in the air. "Your words may be as sweet as honey, but actions speak louder than words. I must protect the King's family and this sacred realm. I shall not spare your life unless you prove your innocence."

His bow was still drawn, and he spelled out the consequence with chilling resolve: "Your life will become a sacrifice, an offering to safeguard the royal kin and prevent any harm to Vessantara's beloved wife and children."

Terrified, the Brahmin found himself trapped in a dangerous predicament, desperately trying to save his life from the hunter's bow and a relentless pack of hounding dogs.

Illustration 6: While dogs chase Jujaka up a tree, the forester bents his bow, aiming directly at him.

The Brahmin responded with a deceptive mix of partial truths and misleading statements, "Noble guard, you must know that an ambassador is considered sacred, inviolate, and under the protection of ancient laws. Harm befalling such a man would bring terrible consequences. The people yearn for King Vessantara's return, and even his parents long for him deeply. I am here as their ambassador, seeking the King's trace, to bear messages of love and longing from his kin. If you know of his dwelling place, I implore you to share it with me."

His words were carefully crafted to evoke sympathy and understanding, hoping to resonate with the forester's sense of duty and compassion. The air hung heavy with uncertainty as the forester deliberated on whether to trust the Brahmin's claims or remain vigilant in his mission to protect the King's secluded abode.

As the words reached the Brahmin's ears, a shiver ran down his spine, and the color drained from his face. His heart raced, and a gnawing fear gripped his soul. His eyes darted around, searching for an escape, a way out of the impending doom he felt closing in.

"The Brahmin is sacred, invulnerable to harm," he stammered, desperation lacing his voice. "A rule as old as time, none may lay a hand on him."

With a heavy heart, he continued, his words weaving a tale of regret and sorrow. "The people's remorse now weighs upon them. His father, a wellspring of grief, his mother's eyes dimmed by tears of agony. Their hearts long for him, aching for his return."

His voice, once confident, now trembled as he spoke with a newfound determination. "Fear not, for I am a messenger, bearing a plea for Vessantara's return. His presence is a balm to soothe the suffering that now engulfs his home."

The Brahmin Jujaka's gaze held a mix of hope and trepidation as he leaned in, his voice lowering to a conspiratorial whisper. "Tell me, kind stranger, if knowledge of his abode lies within you. Guide me to the sanctuary he has sought, and our gratitude shall know no bounds."

His heart was pounding, the Brahmin's words hung in the air, and a tense silence enveloped them both. Then, like a dam breaking, a wave of relief washed over him as the forester's lips curved into a smile. "Oh, rejoice! Your presence is a beacon of hope. Come, let us stow away my dogs and prepare for a journey of revelation."

CHAPTER 6

DEEP WITHIN THE FOREST

The forester gestured towards the Brahmin, inviting him to settle down on a comfortable arrangement of twigs that he had thoughtfully arranged. With a friendly and welcoming tone, he spoke, "Please accept this small gesture of hospitality, dear envoy. I offer you a nourishing meal of succulent roasted deer meat and sweet honey, which will undoubtedly provide sustenance for your long and arduous journey."

As the forester's eyes scanned the vast horizon, his voice took on a new energy. He gestured in the direction of a towering rocky prominence looming in the distance. "See that? Beyond those rugged cliffs lies Gandhamadan, the abode of Vessantara," he exclaimed excitedly.

The forester extended his arm and began to vividly describe the scene before them. "He is dressed in the robe of a Brahmin, and his face has the appearance of a hermit. His once-neat hair is now matted in humble surrender, and his attire is made of simple skins that remind us of the beauty of unadorned life."

His voice carried a sense of reverence as he described the hermitage's surroundings. "The hills abound with trees heavy-laden with luscious fruits. Mangoes, rose apples, jackfruits, and myrobalans are a feast for the senses. Bo and golden tindook, and the banyan's grandeur offer shelter and shade."

His words became poetic as he painted a vivid tapestry of nature's symphony. "Figs, like dancers in the wind, sway to the rhythm of the forest's song. Among the branches, birds unite in the chorus – najjuha, cuckoos, and more – a melody that never tires."

The forester's description of the forest's beauty continued, his voice rich with imagery. "Vines, shrubs, and noble sal trees sway like joyful souls, wherever the breeze may carry its tender touch."

He extended his arm, encompassing the expanse of the landscape. "Peaks kiss the very heavens, their grandeur reaching for the sky. And nestled beneath, a tranquil lake adorned with lilies in hues of blue and white, a vision of celestial elegance."

The forester's words flowed like a river, carrying the listener to a place of wonder. "In this haven of nature's artistry, Vessantara dwells with his children and wife. A

Brahmin's mien he dons, his ascetic path a testament to his noble spirit."

His voice lowered in reverence, capturing the essence of Vessantara's humble life. "A hermit's garb, matted hair, and a spoon that tends to sacred flames. He lies upon the earth's embrace, a testimony to a purposeful existence."

The forester's narrative painted a picture of a lush haven of natural abundance and divine tranquility. "Amidst the forest's embrace, trees laden with fruits offer their bounty. Mangoes, rose apples, and the golden tindook, a feast for those who partake."

With a flourish, he conjured an image of life's vibrant tapestry. "A symphony of colors and scents dance upon the breeze. Ebony, aloe, and trumpet flowers create a vivid mosaic, a canvas painted by nature's masterful hand."

The forester's voice grew animated, his words evoking the pulse of the forest's heart. "Acacias, berries, and nuts thrive, a testament to nature's generosity. A thriving ecosystem where each element finds its purpose, a symphony of life and growth."

A sense of awe enveloped his words as he described the serene tableau before them. "Above, birds create a chorus, their songs echoing through the hills. A symphony of joy, their melodies intertwine with the very fabric of the forest."

The man's description turned poetic as he painted a picture of the hermitage's surroundings. "Honey drips from flowers like tears of joy, adorning the lilies below. Breezes carry the scent of flowers in every direction, a fragrant embrace that dances upon the air."

His words spoke of a place of sustenance for body and mind. "Rice and berries fall like blessings, a gift from nature's hand. Fish, crabs, and tortoises navigate the lake's serene expanse, an ecosystem of harmony."

A reverent pause filled the air before the man's voice resounded, a final flourish to his grand portrait. "Such is the realm where Vessantara resides, his family united. A realm of tranquility and purpose, where life's essence is distilled to its purest form."

With his tale spun, the forester's gaze met the Brahmin's, a shared understanding passing between them. And in that moment, a path was set, a journey awaiting its travelers.

And so, the forester painted the canvas of Vamka Hill, his words weaving a vivid tapestry of nature's bounty. Captivated by his tale, Brahmin Jujaka's face lit up with delight as he took in the serenity of the scene before him. He extended his gratitude through the cadence of a stanza:

"Accept this piece of barley bread,
all soaked with honey sweet,
and lumps of well-cooked honey cake:
I give it to you to eat."

The air carried the sweet scent, and the forest seemed to pause. Responding with a humble demeanor, the countryman declined,

"I thank you for your kindness, sir. Although your offer is well-intentioned, I do not need any provisions as my stores are still plentiful. However, I would like to offer my generosity to you. Please let me know if you need anything. I would be happy to share my food with you so that you can taste it and enjoy it."

With mutual courtesy, the forester guided Jujaka, unveiling the pathway to a hermitage where Accata, the ascetic, resided.

"Straight onward to a hermitage the pathway there will lead, where Accata a hermit dwells, buck-toothed, with dirty head, with Brahmin dress, with hook and spoon, the ascetic's matted hair, skin-clad he lies upon the ground and tends the fire with care."

With a warm nod and a thankful smile, Jujaka accepted the proffered provisions. He now knew the path he must tread, and his heart surged with anticipation. With a determined step, he began to set his journey in motion.

"Thank you, kind friend, for your generosity. May your days be blessed with abundance and peace."

***

The Brahmin Jujaka, now on a quest, followed the path around Ceta towards the right, embarking on a journey filled with anticipation. His heart danced with delight as he approached Accata's abode, an oasis of tranquility in the heart of the woods. The forest seemed to welcome him, its ancient boughs bending to reveal the secrets hidden within its depths.

Upon reaching the hermit's dwelling, Bharadvaja, the Brahmin, greeted Accata with words as gentle as the rustling leaves.

"O holy sage, I hope this day finds you in good fortune's keep, may your life be marked by fruits and roots and slumber deep. Have flies and gnats, those tiny foes, ever marred your reprieve, or fierce predators of the wild, have they ever made you grieve?"

Accata, sensing a visitor, greeted him with a serene smile. "I thank you, Brahmin, for your kind wishes. I am indeed prosperous and well in this woodland sanctuary. Here, amidst nature's bounty, I find grains, roots, and fruits aplenty. The buzzing of flies and the dance of gnats do not disturb my peace; the creeping creatures are my silent companions. Even the wild beasts of prey acknowledge the harmony of this sacred dwelling."

As Accata spoke, his voice carried the wisdom of a sage who had communed with the forest spirits for eons. His eyes held the depth of one who had witnessed the dance of seasons without counting the passing years.

"In the countless years I've resided here," continued Accata, "no harmful sickness has dared to intrude. You, O Brahmin, are a welcomed guest. Blessings guide your steps. Come, rest within this sacred space. Let the water from the hidden cave quench your thirst, and partake of the tindook, piyal leaves, and kasumari, gifts of the forest's bounty."

Jujaka, with a polite nod, accepted the offerings. Yet, his true intentions lurked beneath his courteous demeanor.

"Accepted is your kindness," he said, his words concealing a hidden agenda. "I seek the lost son of Sanjaya, banished by the people of Sivi. If you, noble sage, know of his whereabouts, reveal them to me."

Accata, the wise hermit, sensed the unspoken desires that tainted Jujaka's quest. "You seek the King of Sivi, not with virtuous intent," he replied, his gaze unwavering. "It seems your true desire lies in the son's wife, Kanhajina, or perhaps in Jali, the loyal children. Or is it the mother, along with her innocent children, that you wish to bring forth? He knows no luxuries here, wealth or opulence, my discerning visitor."

Jujaka's countenance betrayed the complexity of his emotions, caught between the consternation of scrutiny and the unwavering purpose of his quest. With a measured response, he acknowledged the ascetic's insight.

"Your words, sage of the woods, carry the weight of truth, a fact I won't contest. Yet, let it be known that my intentions are steadfast, seeking redemption and aid," Jujaka proclaimed, his voice blending sincerity and determination.

Accata, the astute and seasoned observer of human motives, met Jujaka's gaze with an unwavering stare. "Your quest, dear sir, harbors secrets deep, veiled intentions in your plea. Nevertheless, I shall grant the guidance you seek. To Vamka Hill, go and see," he concluded, his eyes reflecting the ancient wisdom of generations past.

Illustration 7: Jujaka approaches the hermit Accata, seeking information about Vessantara's location.

In response to the ascetic's caution, Jujaka's voice assumed a more sincere note. "Please, good sage, do understand; I bear no ill intent. I seek neither favors nor do I wish to impose. My journey is one of discovery, a quest for the truth, to locate this ruler and restore to his realm a fruitful youth."

With wise eyes gained from years of solitude, the ascetic gave a nod of acceptance. "I take you at your word, noble traveler. Let us harbor no mistrust but enjoy a pleasant meeting of souls, akin to the beauty of nature we relish. Though I have not laid my eyes upon the King you seek, truth be told, I shall unfold the path to his dwelling if you so desire."

With a reassuring nod, Accata extended an invitation. "Stay by my side today, partake of the wild roots and fruits with me. As the sun rises bright tomorrow, I shall be your guide to Vamka Hill."

***

As the morning sun painted the sky in hues of gold, the ascetic led the way with a stretched hand, guiding Jujaka through the verdant expanse. Step by step, their journey unfolded like a dance to the rhythm of nature's heartbeat.

And on that day, the ascetic's words found voice once more, narrating the vivid canvas of Vamka hill's beauty:

"The pepper tree's leaves, a resplendent green,
A haven of purity, a paradise serene.
Grass-like the neck of a peacock, vivid and soft,
A lush carpet underfoot, a tender loft.

Kapittha, mango, and rose-apple trees stand,
Nature's bounty in bloom, a fragrant band.
Fig trees hang low, their fruits ripe and sweet,
Perfuming the air, nature's own treat.

Streams, like sapphires, clear and bright,
Fish playfully dance in the shimmering light.
A lake, embraced by the woods, a sight to adore,
Lilies, white and blue, on its mirrored shore.

And close by, another scene of heaven's own grace,
Lilies in three shades, nature's delicate embrace."

The ascetic's words painted a vivid picture, each detail imbued with life and vitality. As the forest path wound on, Jujaka's heart brimmed with anticipation, his senses alive to the wonders awaiting him on the slopes of Vamka hill.

He praised the square-shaped lake with its lilies, then turned to talk about Lake Mucalinda:

(song)

Soft as petals, gentle bloom, colors blue and white,
Lilies dance in grace in Lake Mucalinda's light.
In countless hues, they rise with thrill, winter's icy chill,
Knee-high, they stand, a fragrant thrill, a scene to fulfill.

Oh, the air is sweet with buzzing bees,
Nature's melody, carried by the breeze.
Around the hermit's fire, they twirl and spin,
In nature's embrace, a lively din.

Ebony and trumpet-flower by waterside so grand,
Kadamba trees they stand, in leafy splendor they command.
Six petals or more, a diverse parade,

Leafy bowers intertwined, nature's beauty displayed.

Breezes carry scents of red, white, blue,
Around the fire's glow, nature's wonders in view.
By the waterside, a symphony of sway,
Echoing the bees' hum, a melody's ballet.

Mustard, green garlic, lilies in blue,
Jasmine's sweet embrace, a fragrant debut.
Creepers entwine like a tapestry's loom,
Nature's artistry, in every shade they bloom.

Scents of jasmine and sandalwood's embrace,
Cotton's soft touch, a vibrant space.
Seeds and grasses, reaching for the sky,
A chorus of life, reaching oh so high.

Lions, tigers, elephants in their quest,
Deer and agile fawns, a watery nest.
Yaks, antelopes, monkeys' playful spree,
Bears and mighty creatures, wild and free.

A dance of creatures, a forest's song,
Nature's choir, vibrant and strong.
Birds in chorus, songs in flight,
Under the moon's gaze, a magical night.

Elephants, deer, a woodland grace,
Creepers hanging, a vibrant embrace.
Mustard, sugar-cane, rice in array,
Nature's gifts blooming, in sun's golden ray.

The path leads, to a tranquil space,
Vessantara's haven, a peaceful embrace.
Brahmin's garb, matted hair, so serene,
A life of hermit grace, in nature's scene.

***

The Brahmin Jujaka was a man who was determined to achieve his goals. He had a heart full of hope and purpose, and he was not going to let anything stand in his way. With each stride he took, he could feel himself getting closer and closer to his destination - the dwelling of Vessantara. The journey was long and treacherous, but Jujaka was not discouraged. He knew that his determination and perseverance would lead him to success.

Jujaka had been regaled with tales of Vessantara's boundless generosity and the warmth of his family. Filled with anticipation, the Brahmin longed to meet them and implore Vessantara to bestow upon him the precious gift of his children, all in an effort to bring joy to his own wife. He was not going to let anything stand in his way. With a heart filled with hope and purpose, the Brahmin set forth on a determined stride, his path leading him toward the dwelling of Vessantara.

CHAPTER 7

NARRATIVES OF THE CHILDREN

Brahmin Jujaka followed the trail that was revealed to him by Accata, the hermit. As he walked, the path gradually transformed into a gentle one until it finally opened up to a breathtaking sight. Before him lay the serene expanse of a four-sided lake, its sapphire-blue waters glistening in the sun's warm embrace. The golden rays of the sun cast an enchanting aura upon the surroundings, creating a captivating ambiance. Despite the tranquil beauty of the place, Jujaka's mind was occupied with calculating thoughts. His intentions were far from noble, and he concealed his sinister motives beneath a veneer of poise.

"By now, Maddi should have concluded her forest sojourn," he mused. "Women, with their constant chatter, can impede my purpose. When she ventures back into the woods tomorrow, I shall approach Vessantara and beseech him for the children. I must ensure my departure before her return."

After deciding on his path, Jujaka came across a flat hill nearby. He noticed that the hilltop offered both privacy and a good view. He lay down on the soft earth, surrounded by the embrace of nature, his thoughts wavering between excitement and the tangled web of his scheming. As the day surrendered to the mysteries of the night, he drifted into an uneasy sleep.

***

In dreams, Maddi's mind became a canvas for haunting imagery. In her sad dream, a mysterious figure materialized— a man of dusky complexion clad in flowing yellow robes, the vibrant hue striking against the darkness of his skin. He had fiery red blossoms decorating his ears, strikingly contrasting his outfit. In this surreal encounter, he breached the sanctuary of their leaf-woven hut, his spectral grip seizing Maddi by her raven locks. With inexorable force, he hauled her from the haven of their home, her body yielding to the relentless tug. She lay sprawled on the earth, gazing up at the cruel sky, a mere pawn in an otherworldly game.

Her world plunged into a nightmarish mixture as her captor, heedless of her pleas, executed unspeakable horrors. He seized her eyes, severing her vision from her reality, stripped her of her arms, left her chest rent asunder, and culminated his gruesome act by wresting her heart from her very being, crimson tendrils clinging to his ghostly grasp. Maddi awoke, her heart pounding in tandem with her breaths, her body drenched in cold sweat. The dream's echoes reverberated within her, a symphony of terror.

With tremulous resolve, Maddi pushed her fears aside. "There is no interpreter of dreams but Vessantara," she affirmed, determination fanning the flames of her resolve. Her steps guided her towards the hermitage, where the Great Being resided. Her knuckles rapped softly upon the door, and his voice resonated from within, "Who approaches?" She answered, "It's I, my lord, Maddi." She could sense the undertones of reproach as he replied, "Lady, your visit breaches our agreement."

Fighting the tremor in her voice, Maddi prayed, "My lord, I stand here not by whim but driven by a chilling dream." His tone softened as he granted permission, "Speak, Maddi. Share with me the secrets that haunt your sleep." And so, within the walls of the hermitage, she spun the thread of her vision, painting the portrait of her nightmare in vivid strokes.

Vessantara, with his wisdom unfolded, discerned the hidden meaning beneath the tapestry of her words. "The threads of destiny align," he thought, realizing the moment was at hand for his supreme act of generosity. The realization crystalized—he would soon face a suitor seeking his offspring. Nurturing his own complex plan, he masked his knowledge behind gentle deception.

"Maddi, sometimes sleep's embrace breeds restless visions, a byproduct of the body's rhythms. Let your anxieties find break," he assured her, his words both solace and smokescreen.

Maddi's heart, soothed by his words, was granted the space to mend. With the light of dawn's arrival, she tended to her duties, her embrace wrapping her children in warmth and love. Her voice, laden with maternal care, recounted her haunting dream while her gaze held the weight of unspoken emotions. The children, though innocent, seemed to glean the gravity of her words.

The ritual complete, Maddi reluctantly withdrew her embrace, entrusting her most precious treasures into the care of the Great Being. Wiping the glistening tears from her cheeks, she gathered her resolve, clutching her basket and tools as she stepped into the world beyond, the forest's embrace awaiting her.

***

Yet, Jujaka's calculations were awry. He believed Maddi's departure had paved the way for his conniving stratagem. He descended the hill with measured steps, crossing the footpath that meandered toward the hermitage.

Emerging from his humble abode, Vessantara, the embodiment of serenity, settled upon a weathered stone slab. His presence radiated a tranquil yet anticipatory aura, akin to a wanderer who had long dreamt of quenching his thirst in an oasis.

His children, a pair of innocent souls, encircled around him, weaving a tapestry of innocence and laughter amidst the untamed backdrop of nature. Oblivious to the complexities of adulthood, their hearts danced to the rhythms of joy that life offered. The Great Being's gaze, unwavering and imbued with a deep undercurrent of expectation, remained immersed on the path that was soon to escort the suitor and the destiny he bore.

The passage of time stretched out its minutes, creating a sense of anticipation in every moment. In the distance, the figure of the Brahmin crystallized, each footfall a note in the symphony of preordained fate. Carrying his desires like an intricately carved gemstone, he neared the hermitage—a man transformed, his seven months of renunciation poised to crystallize into a fervent plea. A surge of jubilant recognition swelled within Vessantara as he hailed, his voice ringing out with an exuberant welcome, "Brahmin, draw near!"

Turning his attention to his son, Jali, the Great Being's tone was a fusion of delight and nostalgia. "Jali, my son, rise and bear witness to this Brahmin who approaches us. The wheel of time seems to have wound back, presenting us with a familiar face. My heart is set alight with joy."

Prince Jali, a young embodiment of purity, followed his father's gaze with wide-eyed wonder. His voice, untouched by artifice, resonated with the truth of his observations. "Indeed, father, I perceive the Brahmin of whom you speak. He advances purposefully, as if in quest of a boon that fate has woven into our story. A destined guest he shall be."

With a gracious nod of respect, the young boy gracefully rose from his seat and took measured steps toward the approaching Brahmin. An air of innocence and genuine kindness emanated from him as he extended his offer to assist with the Brahmin's burden. As he drew closer, the Brahmin's eyes fell upon the boy, but his mind turned bitter. "This must be Jali, Vessantara's son," he surmised, making a conscious decision to assume an austere demeanor right from the outset.

Snap! The Brahmin's fingers emitted a sharp crack, accompanied by an imperious command, "Step back, step back!" The boy, momentarily taken aback by this unexpected harshness, couldn't help but form a negative judgment about the Brahmin—a man seemingly devoid of warmth, his exterior marred by the conspicuous eighteen flaws that marked his body.

Unperturbed by the young boy's retreat, the Brahmin approached the Great Being Vessantara, his outward demeanor still steeped in a veneer of politeness. With a well-practiced gesture of respect, he began, "Respected ascetic, may you be in a state of well-being and prosperity. Does this forest generously provide you with an ample supply of grains, roots, and fruits? Have you, in your solitude, encountered the vexations of bothersome flies and gnats or perhaps confronted the threats posed by untamed beasts?"

In his customary composed manner, the Great Being responded, "I extend my gratitude for your kind inquiry. Yes, we are indeed thriving in this idyllic forest, where nature's bounty blesses us with an abundance of grains, roots, and fruits. The droning hum of flies and the persistent bite of gnats, as well as the lurking presence of predatory beasts, are but distant echoes that fail to breach the tranquility of our chosen sanctuary.

For seven months now, we have found contentment in the embrace of this wilderness, seldom encountering another Brahmin such as yourself, who stands before us with an almost ethereal radiance. Adorned in Brahmin attire and carrying emblematic tools, you display a celestial aura—fascinating and captivating.

Please accept our heartfelt welcome, accompanied by the blessings that unfailingly accompany it. I pray you, step forth and grace our dwelling with your presence. Cleanse your feet and partake in the ritual purification if you so wish. Allow me to present to you the finest leaves of tindook and piyal, along with the fragrant offering of kasumari. Luscious fruits, honey-sweet and ripe, await your indulgence. Also, I humbly offer you the refreshing gift of cool water drawn from a concealed sanctuary atop a lofty hill. Should you desire, quench your thirst and be refreshed."

With these words, the Great Being, Vessantara, discerned the significance of the Brahmin's presence amidst the sprawling wilderness. A notion crystallized in his mind—this visit bore a purpose, a tale yearning to be unraveled. In a moment of keen insight, he voiced his curiosity through a stanza:

"Now, I plead, unravel the intent, unveil the enigma,
That guides your steps to this land of towering flora.

What prompts your journey, what concealed drama,
Led you to endeavor into this lush sanctuary, O visitor?"

Jujaka's words flowed forth like an unyielding river, deep and resonant. Each syllable held a weight of determination as he declared, "Much like a ceaseless river that never falters, I stand before you seeking the favor of great significance. I pray you, grant me the custody of your precious children."

Vessantara, the Great Being, absorbed the request with a heart that swelled like a flourishing tide. It was like he offered a purse laden with a thousand gleaming gold coins. A serene smile graced his lips as he replied, "Your wish is received with open arms. I willingly entrust my beloved children to your care. However, I implore you to spend the night here. With the break of dawn, my wife shall return from her forest sojourn, ready to embrace our offspring. She will bathe and embellish them, adorning their innocent forms with fragrant blossoms. And when the tender touch of morning graces the world, you may embark on your journey with them. Take along an ample assortment of fruits and roots, gifts from our sanctuary to nourish you on your path."

Jujaka hesitated, his brows knitting in inspection. "Mighty ruler," he began, "I'm inclined to depart without delay. I hold a lingering fear of potential hindrances that may materialize on the road ahead. It's a well-known fact that women possess a knack for weaving intricate knots of complications, often leading to unforeseen disruptions."

Understanding the subtle concerns that danced behind Jujaka's words, the Great Being Vessantara offered an understanding nod. "If the prospect of encountering my spouse presents unease, despite her gentle and benevolent nature, I respect your wishes. Allow me to suggest an alternative—let my cherished offspring, Jali and Kanhajina, accompany you instead. They shall venture to their grandfather's abode and duly convey your petition."

Jujaka, however, raised an objection, his voice laced with trepidation. "Yet, my lord, I fear for the potential harm that may occur to my possessions. If the King finds out about my venture, he could take strict action against me. Worse yet, he might resort to more dire actions, casting shadows of death or enslavement over my existence. Bereft of wealth and loyal attendants, how could I possibly face my wife's scornful gaze and biting ridicule?"

Vessantara's voice held a soothing resonance as he sought to allay Jujaka's fears. "Rest assured, my friend. When my children, possessing the gift of eloquence and kind hearts, stand in the presence of the generous monarch, renowned for his unwavering commitment to justice and compassion, they shall return bearing treasures of abundance. The ruler's benevolence shall shower upon you, bestowing a wealth of contentment and joy."

But Jujaka's resolve remained unyielding, his expression resolute. "No, my lord, I find myself unable to heed your counsel. My intentions lean towards enlisting your children as devoted servants, catering to the needs of my household."

Patient and unwavering, Vessantara met Jujaka's determination with his own steadfast resolve. "As you wish, let the course align with your preference. However, bear in mind that when my offspring step into the presence of their grandfather, the generous ruler of Sivi, his heart will be moved by their genuine sincerity. He shall undoubtedly adorn you with the treasures of happiness and satisfaction that life can offer."

***

As the harsh and unforgiving words of the Brahmin struck the air, they fell upon the tender ears of Prince Jali and Princess Kanhajina like stones into a tranquil pond, causing ripples of anxiety to spread through their young hearts. Their innocence, once untouched by the harshness of the world, now bore the weight of adult concerns. Like startled fawns, they hastened to distance themselves and the source of this newfound unease. Their steps were quick and agile, driven by a primal instinct to seek refuge from a looming danger.

Taking cover behind a thicket of bushes, they huddled together, their breaths coming in quick gasps. Wide-eyed and trembling, they exchanged a silent exchange of glances, their eyes mirroring the deep uncertainty that had taken root within them. The world around them seemed to have transformed, the once-familiar forest now holding shadows of uncertainty.

Desperation guided their steps, like the invisible hand of fate urging them onward. They moved with a speed of pure instinct, each footfall a testament to their resolve. They ventured further, driven by an instinctual knowledge that the key to safety lay beyond their present boundaries.

***

Their hurried journey led them to the edge of a tranquil lake, its four sides stretching out in an intricate dance of light and water. It was as if the landscape itself recognized their need for sanctuary. With hearts pounding, they made a choice that belied their youth—courage overcame fear, and they waded into the welcoming embrace of the cool water. It was a choice made not out of defiance but out of necessity, a realization that the water's gentle caress could provide a shroud of protection.

Cloaked in the simplicity of their bark garments, Prince Jali and Princess Kanhajina concealed themselves amongst the lily pads, their small forms blending seamlessly with the delicate foliage. The lily pads became their guardians, their refuge from the storm of uncertainty that raged around them. With heads bowed low, they nestled deeper into their sanctuary, their innocent eyes peering through the natural veil surrounding them. Each passing moment felt like an eternity, their ears tuned to the slightest rustle, their hearts drumming in their chests.

Amidst their fear and the tranquil sounds of nature, an old rhyme surfaced in their thoughts, a mournful echo of their distress:

"So Jali and Kanhajina hither and thither ran,
In deep distress to hear the voice of the pursuing man."

∗∗∗

As the echoes of the children's fleeting steps faded into the forest's embrace, Jujaka's mounting frustration found a target in the Great Being himself. His words sliced through the air, laden with accusation and resentment. "Vessantara," he accused, his voice sharp as a blade, "you dared to weave a treacherous web in the presence of innocence. Did you, with subtle gestures, whisper escape into their ears? For they vanished as swiftly as a whisper itself! You, my fine deceiver, have woven a tapestry of trickery that rivals the gods themselves."

Amidst the accusation, a pang of understanding reverberated within the depths of the Vessantara's heart. The Great Beings couldn't deny that his children's disappearance was a response to his unspoken wishes, a testament to their deep connection and unwavering trust in his wisdom. Yet, rather than succumb to tension, Vessantara met Jujaka's gaze with a serenity that bordered on compassion.

"Do not let anger cloud your judgment, dear sir," Vessantara responded, his voice a calming balm in the midst of the storm. "For even when the winds of fate carry our loved ones away, the tide of love forever pulls them back to our shores." With these words, he rose from his seat, the determination in his eyes echoing the unspoken promise of a father's unwavering devotion.

Step by deliberate step, Vessantara moved towards the rear of the humble hut, guided by an invisible thread of connection that bound him to his children. His heart resonated with the rhythm of their existence, which he had nurtured and protected. His footsteps, steady as the beating of his heart, carried him to the very edge of the wilderness.

As he scanned the trail of footprints that bore witness to their flight, a sense of urgency and understanding propelled him forward. His keen senses, honed by a life lived in harmony with the elements, led him unerringly to the banks of the square-shaped lake, its tranquil surface mirroring the mysteries that danced beneath.

With a voice that carried the weight of love and authority, he called out into the silence, "Jali, my dear son!" The words, imbued with a potent mixture of yearning and assurance, echoed across the water's expanse, reaching the hidden recesses where his children had sought refuge.

Responding to his call, the children stirred from their concealment among the lily pads. Their young faces, a portrait of apprehension and hope, turned towards the source of their father's voice. It was a voice that had woven countless tales of wonder, a voice that held the power to quell their fears and illuminate their path.

With a voice that held the timbre of a father's unwavering love, Vessantara recited the following verses that transcended the boundaries of mere words. Each syllable resonated with the depth of his commitment and the vastness of his vision:

"Come, my cherished child, embrace your noble fate,

Follow my path, fulfill my heart, and conquer life's sea's weight.

Be my vessel, my guide, to navigate the sea of birth,

Beyond realms and gods, I'll sail to freedom's realm unearth."

The sorrowful cry of a father echoed across the stillness of the lake, each syllable infused with a potency that transcended mere sound. "Jali, my son!" The voice, a call to arms against the tumultuous currents of uncertainty, resounded with unwavering clarity through the young boy's thoughts. Amid the swirling eddies of apprehension, Jali's resolve solidified like the sturdy trunk of a tree, unyielding to the storms that raged within.

"I shall honor my father's wishes, no matter the storm that approaches," Jali's inner determination unfurled like the unfaltering leaves of a lotus. Lifting his head, he delicately parted the lily leaves that had hidden him.

Jali emerged from his aquatic sanctuary with a sense of purpose borne from deep-rooted love and trust. His steps, a harmonious symphony with the rhythm of his heartbeat, led him to the shore, where his father stood as a beacon of guidance.

Illustration 8: When Vessantara called his children to emerge from their hiding in the lotus pond, Jali listened, emerged from the pond, and fell at his feet.

Emotions churned within him, a disruption of feelings too immense to be confined by words alone. His heart poured forth in silent supplication as he reached his father's side. Tears, unbidden and unrestrained, carved glistening paths down his cheeks. With an earnestness that defied the boundaries of speech, he flung himself at the feet of the Great Being, holding onto his father's ankle as if grounding himself to an unshakable truth.

The Great Being, Bodhisatta, a vessel of wisdom and compassion, recognized the unspoken language of his son's heart. With a tenderness that transcended age and authority, he touched Jali's head gently. The touch, a reassurance woven of warmth and sympathy, carried a promise of unconditional support. In those moments, beneath the vast expanse of the open sky, father and son connected in a communion that words could never encapsulate.

"Where is your sister, my child?" Vessantara's voice, a melody of concern, reached Jali's ears like a comforting whisper. With a quiver in his voice, Jali spoke, his words a testament to the depths of their bond. "Father, in the face of adversity, every being must navigate their own path." The words, a reflection of the shared resolve that bound them, carried the weight of an agreement forged in the crucible of life's challenges.

Vessantara's eyes held a poignant understanding, reflecting the intricate web of trust woven between his children. A mixture of relief and a lingering concern swirled within him. Yet, unwavering in his faith in their bond, he called out with a voice that harmonized with the rhythms of the universe, "Kanha!"

The verses that followed, imbued with a genuine yearning and an unquenchable thirst for liberation, wove themselves into the tapestry of the scene:
"Come, my beloved daughter dear, fulfill my perfect plan,
Guide me as I cross life's sea in freedom and take my stand.
Be my vessel, my guide, to sail through life's vast, endless sea,
Beyond worlds and gods, I'll journey; in liberation, I'll be."

Her thoughts, like a carefully woven tapestry, affirmed her decision. "There's no need for me to dispute my father's will," she resolved within herself. With a determined grace, she emerged from her place of concealment, her heart a heavy burden as she hastened to her father's side. Moving with a sense of urgency, her steps mirrored the racing rhythm of her emotions. Without hesitation, she clasped onto her father's left ankle, her grip firm and unwavering, tears tracing silvery paths down her cheeks.

The tears of father and daughter converged, falling like the soft patter of raindrops onto the Great Being's feet. The shimmering droplets intertwined with the lush green of a lily pad, blending emotions as deep as the forest enveloping them. As he felt the tender touch of their tears upon his skin, Vessantara's heart swelled with a bittersweet ache—a resonance of love and sacrifice.

Gently, he lifted both Jali and Kanhajina into his arms, their embrace an unspoken affirmation of their unity. "My dear Jali," his voice, a gentle caress wrapped around his son like a comforting shroud, "can you not perceive that I have chosen this path willingly, entrusting you with my aspiration? My son, be the harbinger of my dreams."

In that fleeting moment, Vessantara's voice carried a symphony of guidance, a legacy woven of love and duty. With the finesse of a skilled artisan, he judged the worth of his children not as possessions to be sold but as embodiments of his ideals. Turning his attention to his son, he delved into the intricacies of their destinies. "Jali, should you desire the realm of your own autonomy, you must offer the Brahmin a thousand pieces of gleaming gold. Yet, my beloved daughter, your beauty holds a value beyond mere coin. A suitor of common lineage cannot tie you with a simple sum. Only a King with the power to grant a hundred of everything can offer you such. If you wish to unshackle your life, you must bestow upon the Brahmin a hundred male and a hundred female servants, along with a hundred elephants, horses, bulls, and gold pieces."

Amidst the delicate balance of emotions, his words held solace, like a soothing balm to their turmoil. He laid out the path they must traverse, the price of their eventual liberation, not as a burden but as a challenge to be embraced. With each word, he wove a cocoon of reassurance around their hearts, sheltering them from the turbulent uncertainties that lay ahead. A luminous thread of hope was spun, guiding them through the labyrinthine corridors of their fate.

***

With an aura of quiet strength, Vessantara guided his children back to the sanctuary of their hermitage. There, amidst the whispering leaves and the peaceful symphony of nature, they found solace in the familiar. The weight of their impending destiny was tempered by the knowledge that their father's love would forever be their North Star.

As the sun painted the sky in hues of gold and amber, Vessantara took a pot of water—a symbol of life and purity. With a purpose that resonated through the very earth beneath his feet, he beckoned the Brahmin to approach. The water flowed from his hands, an offering to the heavens, a silent plea for enlightenment that transcended mortal desires. His voice, an earnest whisper, carried a declaration that echoed through the ages, "Omniscience is dearer to me than my own son, a hundredfold, a thousandfold, a hundred thousandfold!"

With hands uplifted in a posture of devotion, Vessantara consecrated this ultimate sacrifice. In a gesture that stretched beyond time itself, he bestowed his most cherished treasures upon the Brahmin—a gift of immeasurable worth, the legacy of a father's boundless love.

In the midst of nature's embrace, Vessantara felt triumphant yet bittersweet. His offering was not a mere transaction but a testament to the boundless love that tethered parent and child. His tender yet steadfast gaze rested upon his children like a blessing woven with threads of pride and longing. As they stood before him, their intertwined destinies now extended beyond the mere confines of their physical beings.

***

Meanwhile, Jujaka, embodying the antithesis of compassion, ventured deeper into the heart of the jungle. With the heartless precision of a predator, he plucked a creeper from its verdant sanctuary; its supple tendrils soon transformed into a cruel symbol of bondage. The children, united by the harsh embrace of the creeper's cord, bore the weight of their shared fate. The boy's right hand was shackled to the girl's left, a twisted manifestation of the Brahmin's ruthless intent.

The cruel dance of their ordeal commenced—a symphony of pain and despair. The Brahmin's staff, an instrument of agony, descended with relentless force upon their small, tender frames. Like vipers' fangs, the creeper's ends struck their delicate skin, leaving trails of crimson anguish in their wake. Their very souls cried out against the injustice of their plight.

Bound as they were, the children struggled to find balance, their steps faltering as they sought to cross the torturous path set before them. They leaned upon each other in their interdependence, drawing strength from their shared agony. Then, as fate often intervenes in the most unexpected of moments, the Brahmin stumbled. His fall upon the unforgiving earth offered a fleeting sliver of providence—a momentary relief from their torment.

In a breath stolen from despair, the children seized the opportunity bestowed upon them by the hands of fate. Like young fledglings yearning for the sky's embrace, they wriggled free from the creeper's grasp, their movements swift and desperate. Their bonds relinquished, they fled from the clutches of their tormentor, their eyes blurred by tears, their hearts a symphony of trepidation and hope.

With feet fleet as the wind, they retraced their steps through the verdant web of the forest, back to the comforting refuge of their father's hermitage. Their journey was not merely one of distance but of destiny realized—a return to the sheltering arms of love's sanctuary.

***

Jali, the young boy, rushed forward with a fervor born of desperation, his tears intermingling with the earth's dust upon his cheeks. His arms found refuge around his father's feet, an emotional embrace that spoke volumes in its silence. The Great Being, towering above him, met his son's gaze with a mixture of compassion and inquiry. Kanha, too, stood nearby, her countenance a mirror of her brother's turmoil.

Quivering with emotion, Jali begged his father, his voice a tender plea, "Father, as mother wanders in the embrace of the forest, can you weave our destiny with your compassionate hands? I beg you to withhold our fate until her return graces us. Only then can we bear the Brahmin's cruel plans when she stands beside us. He may sell us as slaves or even extinguish our lives without a shred of remorse."

The threat of the Brahmin haunted Jali's words, his description vivid and unsettling—a malevolent entity adorned in fearsome attributes. His form, akin to a grotesque goblin, was etched in the boy's memory— sagging flesh, a nose twisted from malice, and eyes that gleamed with an eerie light. A portrait of hostility, the Brahmin's visage bore the mark of a heart devoid of empathy.

Like a plea to the heavens, Jali's words echoed with a question that pierced the depths of his father's soul. "Can you, dear father, stand idly by as this monstrous figure lays claim to our lives? Does your heart remain impervious to our plight as he chains us like cattle, driving us away with a callous indifference?"

Vessantara's gaze held a gravitas, a solemn acknowledgment of his son's agonizing query. The silence that followed was laden with meaning—a pause in which emotions intertwined, a tapestry of love, duty, and the relentless currents of destiny.

With a voice as steady as the forest's ancient trees, the Great Being began to unspool his response, every word a testament to his wisdom and compassion. "My dear Jali, fear not. Your father's guiding hand will navigate you through the storm even as the tempest rages. Your mother's return will herald a new chapter, one in which our shared fate will unfold."

With measured steps, he moved toward the children, his presence a soothing balm against the harsh world outside. His touch, as gentle as the whisper of the wind through leaves, was a gesture of solace, a reassurance that they were not alone in their struggle. "My children," he said, his voice a river of calm, "there is a path that lies before us, a path paved with sacrifice and love. I have assigned a value, not to your hearts, but to the means through which your freedom shall be won."

The Great Being, Bodhisatta's words were not a proclamation of defeat but a declaration of the strength that lay dormant within them. As he laid bare the price of their freedom, he wove an invisible thread of courage and determination, an unspoken promise that they were equal to the challenge.

In the tranquil heart of the forest, the Great Being stood as a sentinel of time, his thoughts a symphony of emotions that danced beneath his composed exterior. The weight of his decision lay heavy upon him, an unspoken sacrifice that echoed through the very fabric of his being. His gaze, fixed upon the horizon, seemed to pierce the veil between the mortal realm and the ethereal, a contemplative connection to a realm beyond.

Amidst this poignant silence, a voice emerged from the depths of sorrow, a voice that held within its tender cadence the essence of a child's heartache. Jali began to weave his lament upon the canvas of existence, his eyes shimmering with unshed tears, his young soul heavy with a burden that belied his years.

"I'm not a stranger to the agony of death's sharp sting," he began, his words a fragile melody that hung in the air like a wisp of smoke, "for it's a destiny we all must ultimately embrace. But what rends my spirit and casts shadows upon my dreams is the haunting specter of my parents' vacant gaze."

Jali's voice carried a depth of emotion that flowed like a river of empathy, carving its way through the hearts of all who listened. His words were not a mere expression of fear; they were a raw confession of the profound love that bound their souls. "The love that once kindled their eyes," he continued, his voice a whisper that held the power to move mountains, "now stands as a phantom, a memory of tenderness lost in the vast expanse of our fate."

***

A somber hush fell upon the forest as Jali's lament echoed among the trees, each syllable a poignant reminder of the intricacies of human existence. The trees themselves, ancient sentinels of time, seemed to sway in rhythm with the boy's sorrow as if nature itself mourned the inevitability of change.

Although tinged with sorrow, Jali's voice carried a note of resilience—an acknowledgment of the pain that awaited his parents, yet also an affirmation of the strength that would take them forward. "Endless nights and days of sorrow lie ahead," he confessed, a gentle caress that touched the hearts of mortals and spirits, "Their tears will trace a map of grief, a river of memories that can never be erased."

The boy's voice quivered as he conjured the image of his sister, Kanha, a radiant presence now absent from their lives. "Kanhajina," he murmured, the syllables carrying the weight of longing, "she who bloomed like the rose-apple trees by the lake, her absence will be a silence that resounds in their souls, a void that no breeze can fill."

Amidst the sad tapestry of his words, Jali's voice took on a cadence of gratitude, a recognition of the bountiful gifts bestowed upon them by the forest. "The fig and jackfruit trees, the mighty banyan that stands like a sentinel," he recounted, his words an homage to the natural world that cradled their existence, "Every treasure of the woods, we leave behind as we step into the unknown."

With a tenderness that seemed to transcend his years, Jali's voice wove a tapestry of memories—their joyful playgrounds by the river's edge, the sweetness of ripe fruits that lingered upon their tongues, and the echoes of laughter that once danced upon the hill. "These cherished moments," he confessed, his voice a fragile echo of times gone by, "like fragile petals, we leave behind today, an offering to the symphony of life."

And then, like a whispered promise to the toys that had once kindled their youthful spirits, Jali's voice carried a final refrain—a pledge that even as they embarked upon a journey of uncertainty, the treasures of their past would forever remain enshrined in the temple of their hearts. "Horses, oxen, elephants," he whispered, his voice a reverent hymn to innocence and joy, "we relinquish them without a tear, for they are but tokens of a childhood that will forever dwell within us."

As Jali's lament trailed off, a profound stillness settled over the forest, a silence that seemed to echo the resonance of his words. The trees stood as ancient witnesses to the ebb and flow of human existence, their leaves rustling in whispered agreement. And amidst this sacred hush, the Great Being stood, his heart a tapestry woven with threads of love, sacrifice, and the unbreakable bond between parent and child.

***

As they crossed the familiar paths of their forest abode, the beauty of their surroundings seemed to take on an even more profound significance, every tree and leaf whispering a silent farewell.

Jali, his young heart brimming with a sense of responsibility, turned to his father, his voice a reflection of the love and gratitude that flowed between them. "Dear father," he began, his words a gentle caress upon the air, "as we embark upon this unknown path, my heart is heavy with the thought of leaving you behind. But I carry the lessons you've engraved upon my soul."

Kanhajina, her gaze a mirror of her brother Jali's emotions, added her voice to the conversation. "Indeed, father," she spoke softly, her words a soothing melody amidst the uncertainty, "please convey to our beloved mother the ache that resides within our hearts, the void her absence has created."

Jali's voice held a note of yearning as he continued, "May the winds that sweep through these ancient woods carry our messages of longing to her ears, and may they bring her the warmth of our embrace." His eyes, clear and sincere, held a reflection of the unconditional love that bound their family.

Kanhajina's voice joined her brother in a symphony of hope and well-wishes. "In the tapestry of life that you continue to weave, dear father," she spoke, her words like a gentle breeze that rustled the leaves, "may threads of happiness and joy be mingled, creating a canvas that radiates with the hues of contentment."

Jali, his thoughts drifting to the treasures they once frolicked with under the sun's embrace, shared his aspirations. "And the companions of our innocent laughter," he spoke, a wistful smile tugging at his lips, "the oxen that carried us upon their strong backs, the horses that galloped beside us, and the elephants that stood as gentle giants—they too shall find solace in your care."

Kanhajina's eyes held a quiet understanding, her voice a whispered promise. "With each step they take, may their hooves etch a message of comfort upon the earth," she shared, her words carrying a tender hope, "a message that tells our mother we remember, we miss her, and we yearn for her return."

As they moved forward, the forest bearing witness to their conversations, Jali's voice returned, a refrain of fond remembrance. "Those creatures of laughter and play," he continued, his voice a soothing presence amidst the inevitable ache of parting, "let them grace her days with their gentle presence, and in their familiarity, may she find a moment of respite from her sorrows."

Kanhajina's gaze met her brother's; their hearts united in their intentions. "Oxen, horses, elephants," she whispered, her voice carrying a subtle melody of nostalgia and hope, "let them become emissaries of joy, a reminder that the bond between mother and child transcends distance and time."

***

The hermitage was cloaked in an air of somber stillness as if the weight of the universe had descended upon its leafy confines. Within its humble walls, Vessantara stood as a monument of sorrow. His once-proud shoulders sagged under the burden of his children's plight, his heart a raging storm of anguish. The core of his being seemed to tremble, a reflection of the uncontrollable quiver of his limbs.

His spirit, which had endured ascetic trials and tested the limits of human endurance, was now gripped by an emotional maelstrom. He was an elephant caught in the relentless jaws of a fierce lion, unable to break free, or the moon veiled by Rahu's shadow during an eclipse. His mighty resolve, often as unshakeable as the mountains, now wavered like a flame buffeted by a storm.

In this moment of profound despair, Vessantara sought refuge within the sanctuary of his hut. Its leafy walls bore witness to his tears, to the raw outpouring of grief from a father's anguished heart. The shadows danced upon the walls, mirroring the tumultuous dance of emotions within him.

"Vessantara, the noble Prince, gave his gift away with care,
Within his leafy sanctuary, he grieved in deep despair."

The verses that resonated through the hush were a haunting melody, a lament born from the depths of a father's soul. Heavy with meaning, each word reverberated with the ache of his heart.

"O, when my children cry for food at morn or eventide,
When hunger and thirst oppress their souls, who will their needs provide?
Their tiny feet, so tender, how will they journey on,
Without shoes to shield them as they tread the paths anon?
How could that Brahmin show no shame while I stood there, stunned,
To strike my innocent children so, a deed that makes my heart aghast?
No person with an ounce of shame would act so cruelly,
Not even to a lowly slave, nor a servant such as me.
Though I can't see them in that plight, I hear them cry and fear,
While trapped like fish, I stand here helpless, wiping away my tears."

Each verse, like a dagger, pierced the air, carrying with it the weight of a father's worst fears. His mind conjured images of his children's suffering, the pain of their hunger, and the torment of their innocence being crushed beneath the Brahmin's callousness. It was a torment that clawed at his heart, the ache of powerlessness gnawing at his very core.

And yet, amidst his emotions, a flicker of resolve emerged. With each tear that fell, with each note of his lament, Vessantara's thoughts churned. Revenge, swift and fiery, seemed like a tempting option to wrench his children from the jaws of suffering. But as the storm subsided, his wisdom prevailed.

"Sword at his side and bow in hand, he stood prepared for strife,

To bring his children back, he thought and end their woe and strife.

But even if they face demise, to grieve is not the way,

For one who knows the righteous path and seeks a gift today?"

As the echoes of his lament slowly faded, a profound calm settled within him. His gaze turned inward, seeking the counsel of his own moral compass. The path of righteousness, he realized, was not paved with vengeance but with a steadfast commitment to his own principles. To regret a gift, even in the face of hardship, was to compromise the very essence of his noble being.

The forest bore witness to a heart-wrenching scene with each step they took. Jujaka, his malevolence unchecked, continued to lash at the children, his cruel blows falling upon them like a relentless storm. The boy, his voice a vessel for the weight of their shared agony, uttered his lament:

"How often have we heard the truth in words that people say,

Without a mother, we are like orphans on life's way.

Life seems empty now, and death feels better, don't you see?

This cruel, greedy, violent man treats us like a cow to be.

We leave behind the rose-apple trees around the peaceful lake,
And all the beauty of the woods, dear sister, we forsake.
Fig, jackfruit, banyan trees, and every tree that's near,
All the fruits that once were ours, dear sister,
we leave here.
A pleasant park stands over there; the river's cool and clear,
The place where we would laugh and play, dear sister,
we leave here.
The fruits we used to savor once, the flowers that we'd
wear,
They bloom upon the hilltop now, dear sister, we must
share.
And all the little toys we loved, the horses, and the rest,
O Kanha, we say goodbye and leave them with a heavy
chest."

The forest, usually a haven of serenity, now absorbed the echoes of the boy's poignant words. Each syllable hung in the air, a testament to the profound connection between brother and sister, a bond fortified by shared moments and the weight of impending separation.

Amidst the turmoil, the boy's voice carried a potent mix of sorrow and defiance. His words were not just an expression of their loss but a declaration of the unbreakable spirit that still flickered within them. The children clung to their shared memories like a lifeline even as the Brahmin's blows rained down upon their vulnerable forms.

In the boy's lament, the forest itself seemed to mourn, each tree swaying in sympathy, the leaves rustling as if whispering words of consolation. The rose-apple trees, which had witnessed their laughter and dreams, now cast long shadows upon their path as if reaching out to embrace them one last time.

The fig, jackfruit, and banyan trees stood like solemn sentinels, bearing witness to the children's heartache. And the river, once a source of joy, flowed with a subdued murmur as if mourning the innocence that was being stripped away.

***

Time passed with each step as their journey continued into the unforgiving heart of the forest—the terrain, rugged and unwelcoming, tested even the Brahmin's resolve. A moment's lapse in his grip on the rope, a mere flicker of uncertainty, caused the lifeline of his control to slip through his fingers. The children, sensing a glimpse of freedom like startled birds suddenly released from captivity, seized their opportunity and fled.

"Jali and Kanhajina, once led by the Brahmin's hand,
Managed to break free and dashed off, leaving him unmanned."

In the space between heartbeats, the forest bore witness to a scene of fleeting liberation. Their small forms, fueled by a potent mixture of fear and resolve, sprinted towards the only safety they knew – the embrace of their father. Their innocent flight was a stark contrast to the Brahmin's enraged pursuit, his anger stoked like a roaring inferno.

Quickly, Jujaka regained his footing, his pursuit a whirlwind of rage and desperation. Armed with his cord and a stick, his resolve ignited like a firestorm. "Running away, are you?" his voice twisted with malicious triumph, "I won't let you escape!" He caught up to them, his hands closing around their fragile wrists, the cruel bindings sealing their fate once again.

"The Brahmin with his staff and rope, he caught them once again,
With beating, led them back, while their father felt the pain."

Their return was marked by the sting of their captor's blows; the children were thrust back into the cold reality of their predicament. The forest, their silent witness, held the weight of their dashed hopes and the agony of their father's helplessness. Amidst the shadows and sunlight filtering through the trees, their plight unfolded like a tragic tale.

As they were once more led away, Kanhajina's voice broke the silence, her words a plea infused with sadness and a burning sense of injustice.

Then Kanhajina spoke, saying:
"'Father, can't you see?
This Brahmin treats me like a slave, as if I'm not truly free.
A brahmin should be virtuous and live a righteous life,
But he seems like a monster, disguised as a Brahmin, causing strife.
Could you watch us suffer, led by this creature of fright,
To be devoured by a goblin? Father, it's not right!'"

Her voice, a fragile melody amidst the cacophony of the forest, echoed with a mixture of despair and determination. It carried the weight of their shattered expectations, the weight of a child grappling with the stark contrast between their ideals and the grim reality that surrounded them. As they continued their harrowing journey, Kanhajina's words lingered like a haunting refrain, a question posed not just to her father but to the universe itself – a question that resonated with the struggle for justice, compassion, and the enduring power of familial love.

***

In the heart of the forest, as the sun's golden rays painted intricate patterns through the foliage, a poignant scene unfolded. Kanhajina's sorrowful cries resonated like haunting melodies, echoing through the ancient trees. Her father, the Great Being, stood there like a pillar of compassion, his soul tethered to her every word.

As his daughter's lamentations intertwined with the rustling leaves, the Great Being was enveloped by deep sorrow. It was as if a tempest of anguish flowed within him, threatening to tear him apart. His very core burned with intensity, the weight of his emotions escaping in ragged breaths that seemed to scorch his lips. Tears flowed from his eyes, each drop a testament to the depths of his heartache, as though his very essence was being poured out.

Yet, even amid this turbulence of grief, a realization dawned upon him like a glow of light piercing through the storm clouds. His anguish was not a sign of weakness; it was a testament to his boundless love for his children. With this understanding, a surge of strength coursed through him, and he drew upon the wellspring of his wisdom to temper the flames of sorrow. Slowly, he lowered himself to the earth, his gaze fixed on his children, an anchor amidst the tempest.

Meanwhile, the path ahead wound through the rugged terrain, leading deeper into the embrace of the mountains. Kanhajina's cries, like fragile echoes of her inner turmoil, continued to fill the air, carried by the gentle breeze that whispered secrets through the leaves.

"My little feet are weary, the path is hard to bear,
The Brahmin drives us ruthlessly, the sun begins to wear.
We call upon the hills and woods, the creatures that reside,
We bow to forest spirits all, as we pass by their side.
Beseeching them to grant our wish, to keep our mother well,
But still, the Brahmin spurs us on, no kindness does he tell.
If only she could follow us, let her not delay,
The path that leads to the hermit's home, where we are led away."

Amidst the symphony of their anguished voices, their words reached out like fragile tendrils, seeking solace in the midst of turmoil. The forest, ancient and wise, bore witness to this poignant exchange, the very essence of nature attuned to their suffering.

Their voices danced with the breeze, their words a gentle plea to the spirits that guarded these woods, a whispered prayer for their mother's well-being. Kanhajina's voice held a fierce determination, her pleas punctuated by each step that carried her further from the life she knew.

"Thou gatherer of roots and fruits, with hair that's tied in strands,
Seeing the empty hermitage, you'd wring your helpless hands.
Our mother must have gathered much, from her quest in the wild,
Not knowing that a cruel man, both greedy and reviled,
Now binds us like we're cattle, forced to follow single-file."

Kanhajina's words painted a vivid tapestry of their mother's dedication and her tireless efforts to sustain their family even in the face of adversity. She spoke of a life woven with threads of compassion and sacrifice, a stark contrast to the cruelty they now faced.

"Ah, if our mother met him and offered him some food,
A mixture of honeyed fruits, a gesture kind and good,
He wouldn't drive us mercilessly after being fed so well,
Yet cruelly, he drives us on, like tales the shadows tell!"

The forest seemed to hold its breath, the leaves stilling as the weight of their words settled upon the ancient trees. Through their voices, a yearning for a different outcome, a glimmer of hope, was engraved into the very fabric of the woods.

Their lament echoed like a plea, a touching reminder that the bonds of family and love remained unbreakable even in the depths of despair. And so, amidst the towering trees and the gentle susurrus of leaves, their voices carried forth – a testament to their courage, resilience, and unyielding spirit.

***

As the golden sun began its descent towards the horizon, its warm embrace casting long shadows upon the forest floor, a moment of profound significance unfolded. The King, his heart heavy yet resolute, watched as his beloved children were handed over to the Brahmin. In this act of giving, a ripple of cosmic resonance surged forth, its impact resonating far beyond the terrestrial realm. The very fabric of existence seemed to shiver with the weight of this sacrifice, its tremors echoing through realms known and unknown.

CHAPTER 8

THE NARRATIVE ABOUT MADDI

The lamentations of the children, their sad cries that bore witness to the depth of their separation, echoed through the earth's very core. The ethereal corridors that connected human existence to the celestial abodes carried these anguished notes, reaching even the celestial realm of Brahma. The heavenly beings residing upon the snow-capped peaks of the Himalayas, wrapped in their divine contemplations, were stirred from their reverie. With furrowed brows and empathetic hearts, they listened, for the cries of innocence and the pangs of love are a language understood by all, be they mortals or gods. Their eyes turned toward the earthly realm, and a silent vow was made to protect and guide those whose hearts were pure.

Illustration 9: To shield Maddi from the heart-wrenching cries of her children and prevent her return, divine beings take the form of wild beasts, blocking her path.

These celestial beings, touched by the profound emotions courting through the forest, shared a collective understanding. They knew the turbulence that awaited Maddi, the beloved mother of the precious children. "She must not arrive in time to witness this parting," they whispered amongst themselves. "For her love is fierce and boundless, her determination unyielding. She would question Vessantara and unravel this plan. Her grief would be a tempest, and she might venture forth in search of her children, regardless of the dangers that lie ahead."

The three celestial beings, each embodying the majesty and power of the forest's most formidable creatures, made their choice in a divine accord. "Let us take the forms of lion, tiger, and leopard," they decreed, their voices a symphony of cosmic wisdom. "As sentinels, we will ensure her safe passage through our kingdom, shielding her from harm and guiding her journey with the moon's gentle glow."

Thus, the transformation took place. The lion, its golden mane shimmering like a crown of fire, positioned itself in her path. With stripes like obsidian rivers, the tiger assumed its stance solemnly. The leopard, its spotted coat, and a constellation of shadows completed the trio. Their eyes held the wisdom of ages, and their purpose was unwavering.

As Maddi's steps carried her closer to the threshold of her destiny, her path intersected with these magnificent forms. The forest seemed to hold its breath, a hushed reverence permeating the air. She met their gaze, and a current of understanding passed between them, a silent covenant formed in that fleeting moment.

"Daughter of earth, do not fade," their collective presence seemed to convey. "Journey onward, for you are shielded by the guardians of this realm. Let the moonlight guide you, and may your heart find solace in knowing that your children are enveloped in the tapestry of a greater design."

In the ethereal tapestry of the forest's embrace, the gods heeded the call of their divine command. With a whisper of cosmic intent, they shed their celestial forms, becoming one with the primal spirits of the wilderness. The lion, its mane ablaze with twilight hues, settled its majestic form upon the forest path. Beside it stood the tiger, its sleek elegance exuding a quiet strength. Completing this enigmatic trio was the leopard, its spotted coat shimmering like stardust.

***

Meanwhile, Maddi's heart stirred with an inexplicable sense of foreboding as the sun cast its first golden rays upon the verdant realm. The threads of a dream, fleeting yet potent, had woven their way into her consciousness. A dream of shadows and whispers, of paths unseen and destinies entwined. Such dreams often carried deeper truths, and she knew she must heed its silent counsel.

"Last night," she pondered aloud, her voice a mere whisper against the forest's symphony. "Last night, a dream visited me, painting the canvas of my slumber with a disquieting tale. A tale that stirs my soul to action."

With determination flowing through her veins, she embraced the cloak of her mission. Gathering her tools, she ventured forth into the heart of the forest, her steps a ballet upon the earth. Yet, the entire reality seemed to shiver, as if the fabric of the universe had been momentarily disrupted. Her fingers, skilled and sure, faltered, and her spade slipped from her grasp. A cascade of roots and fruits spilled from her basket, their vibrant hues a stark contrast against the shadowy undergrowth.

Her right eye, that fateful omen of unseen forces, throbbed with an insistent ache. Fruit-bearing trees, once lush with abundance, now stood barren and desolate. Barren trees, their branches gaunt and lifeless, bore the phantom weight of imaginary fruits. The forest had become a labyrinth of paradoxes, with blurred boundaries between reality and illusion.

As the sun embarked on its westward journey, casting long shadows that painted the path in hues of twilight, Maddi found herself facing a new challenge. The wilderness she had traversed countless times seemed to transform into an enigma of wildness. Her heart quickened with anxiety, for her husband and her children awaited her return at the hermitage. Jali and Kanhajina, those tender souls who held her heart in their tiny hands, stood like yearning saplings, their longing mirroring that of young calves awaiting the return of their nurturing mother.

In this moment of tender vulnerability, Maddi's voice resonated with a plea that transcended the boundary between human and beast. With reverence in her tone, she addressed the noble creatures who shared this realm. "Kings of the woods, guardians of the wild, hear my plea, for it is born of the sincerest heart. Grant me safe passage, I pray you, that I may traverse this forest without peril."

Her words danced upon the gentle winds, weaving a melody of hope and supplication. She invoked Sita, the epitome of devotion and love, whose steadfast heart had guided her through trials untold. In the delicate dance of her voice, Maddi's plea took root in the hearts of the forest's inhabitants, for the call of a mother's love is a language understood by all living beings.

"Let my steps be unhindered," she implored, her voice as soft as the rustle of leaves in a breeze. "Just as you return to your young ones at day's end, I too long to embrace my children once more. Grant me this boon, and I shall share the bounty of this land with you. Half of my harvest shall be a gift to your realm."

During this brief moment between day and night, humanity and animals became one in a divine agreement. The forest's inhabitants, moved by her genuine plea, granted her passage, their ethereal voices a harmony of benevolence. The gods, recognizing the hour and the fulfillment of their cosmic design, withdrew their guardianship. The lion, the tiger, and the leopard, the embodiment of majesty and grace, gracefully relinquished their stations, their mission fulfilled.

***

The twilight cast long shadows across the hermitage as Maddi returned from her daunting encounter with the wild beasts. A hush fell over the surroundings as the nocturnal symphony began. It was the night of the full moon, a celestial orb bathing the landscape in an ethereal glow. Maddi traversed the covered walk with her heart burdened by fatigue and the anticipation of her children's familiar joy. This path, once adorned with the laughter and playful skips of Jali and Kanhajina, now echoed with a painful silence.

Her voice, usually resonant with the melodies of maternal delight, rang out in the stillness of the night. "The children, dusty, close to home, are wont to meet me here like calves that seek the mother-cow, like birds above the mere. Like little deer with pricked-up ears, they meet me on the way: with joy and happiness, they skip and frolic in their play. But Jali and Kanhajina, I cannot see today."

The covered walk, once witness to the innocence of her children, now stood as a poignant reminder of their absence. Maddi's eyes searching the familiar surroundings expressed the yearning of a mother's heart. "As goat and lioness may leave their young, a bird her cage, to seek food, so have I done their hunger to assuage. But Jali and Kanhajina, I cannot see today."

Her gaze lingered on the traces left by the playful duo—little heaps of earth, a testament to the joyous moments frozen in time. "Here are their traces, close by home, like snakes upon the hill, the little heaps of earth they made all round, remaining still. But Jali and Kanhajina, I cannot see today."

With every word, Maddi's pain resonated in the stillness. The hermitage, once a sanctuary of familial love, now echoed with the haunting absence of her children. "All covered up with dust to me, my children used to run, sprinkled with mud, but now I can see neither one. Like kids to welcome back their dam, they ran from home away as from the forest I returned; I see them not today."

Her voice, a poignant melody of sorrow, wove through the memories of shared moments. "Here they were playing, here this yellow vilva fruit let fall: but Jali and Kanhajina, I cannot see today. These breasts of mine are full of milk; my heart will break withal. But Jali and Kanhajina, I cannot see today."

The hermitage, once resounding with the laughter and footsteps of her children, now stood in stark contrast to the void within Maddi's heart. "They used to cling about my hips, one hanging from my breast: how they would meet me, dust-begrimed, at the time of evening rest! But Jali and Kanhajina, I cannot see today."

As Maddi traversed the landscape of memories, the hermitage became a haunting scene of absence. "Once upon a time, this hermitage became our meeting ground, but now I see no children here; the whole place spins around. My children must be dead! The once-silent place is now devoid of any sound; even the ravens and birds have gone quiet."

In the embrace of the night, Maddi's lament echoed through the stillness, a heart-wrenching ballad of a mother's love confronted by the cruel emptiness of loss.

***

The moon hung low in the night sky, casting an ethereal glow upon the hermitage as Maddi approached the Great Being, her heart heavy with a burden of sorrow. She carried a basket of fruit in her arms, its weight paling compared to the ache within her. As she neared, she beheld the sight of Vessantara, seated in somber silence, devoid of the usual laughter and playful chatter of children.

Her voice trembled with both concern and a growing dread. "Why are they silent? How that dream comes to my thoughts again: the birds and ravens make no sound, my children must be slain! Oh, sir, have they been carried off by some wild beast of prey? Or in the deep deserted woods have they been led astray? Do the little ones sleep? Are they on errands? Have they wandered afar in frolic or in play? I cannot see their hands and feet; I cannot see their hair. Was it a bird that swooped? Or who has carried them away?"

Maddi's words hung in the air, a haunting melody of a mother's anguish. The Great Being, shrouded in his thoughts, offered no reply. Her desperation grew, and she pled, "My lord, why do you not speak to me? What is my fault?" Her voice, a fragile thread of vulnerability, carried the weight of her deepest fears. "It's like the pain of being hit by an arrow, even more bitter because today I cannot see Jali and Kanhajina! This is a second blow to my heart that you have given me, that I cannot see my children, and that you have nothing to say."

The air thickened with the unspoken pain that lingered between them. Maddi, her voice now edged with both sorrow and accusation, uttered words that cut through the silence. "My lord, since you refuse to speak, I fear my days are numbered. You will witness my death tonight."

In the quiet solitude of the hermitage, the Great Being Vessantara coped with the anguish that gnawed at him—the void left by the absence of his children. Seeking to shield his own wounded heart, he decided to wrap his pain in the armor of stern words. With a heavy heart, he recited a stanza to Maddi, the royal Princess whose life had taken a stark turn:

"Oh Maddi, born as a royal Princess, your greatness is renowned. You went out for food early in the morning, so why are you returning so late?"

Maddi, her presence marked by a weariness that transcended the physical, met his gaze. Her response carried the weight of the untold challenges she had faced in the wild. "Did you not hear the lion and the tiger loudly roar when by the lake their thirst to slake they stood upon the shore? As I walked in the woods, there came the sign I knew so well: my spade fell from my hand, and from my arm, the basket fell."

With a tone of vulnerability, she continued, recounting the dangerous encounter with the wild. "Then hurt, alarmed, I worshipped all the quarters, one by one, praying that good might come of this, my hands outstretched in prayer. And that no lion and no pard, hyena, wolf, or bear might tear or harry or destroy my daughter or my son. A lion, tiger, and a pard, three ravening beasts, laid wait and kept me from my homeward path: so that is why I'm late."

As the night draped its shadows over the hermitage, an air of silence enveloped the Great Being. His stoic demeanor spoke volumes, and Maddi, sensing the weight of his unspoken sorrow, waited in the quietude. The profound stillness lingered until the first rays of dawn heralded a new day.

With the sunrise, Maddi, unable to contain the depths of her emotions any longer, began to weave her lament. Her lament, a melodic tapestry of love and anguish, echoed through the sanctuary of the hermitage:

"In the shadows, tended day and night,
Like a pupil to a teacher, seeking what is right.
Clad in goatskins, ventured into the wild,
Seeking roots and fruits for my family's smile.
Yellow vilva for you, my little ones so dear,
Ripe woodland fruits, to bring you joy and cheer.
Lotus root and stalk, a golden-yellow hue,
Join us, O Prince, share this feast with you.
Yellow lilies for your girl, blue for Jali's grace,
In garlands, they dance, call them to this place.
Mighty monarch, hear the delightful sound,
As Kanhajina sings, settling all around.
Banished, joy and woe, in common, we have known,

Answer me, Kanhajina. Has Jali ever shown up?
How many Brahmins have I offended sore,
Of holy life and virtue, sacred lore.
Jali and Kanhajina, I cannot see you today,
In this uncertain journey, where have they strayed?

Maddi's words, a symphony of maternal love and longing, encapsulated the heartache of a mother separated from her cherished children.

Throughout the night, as the velvety shroud of darkness draped itself over the land, the Great Being remained enshrouded in silence. His countenance, illuminated by the moon's tender glow, held an aura of both solemnity and contemplation. Time passed in suspended anticipation, the world seemingly holding its breath in reverence for the unfolding drama of hearts entwined with fate.

With the first tendrils of dawn reaching across the sky like gentle fingers, the atmosphere seemed to ripple with a palpable undercurrent of sorrow. Maddi, standing like a solitary figure in the theater of nature, began to weave her feelings into words, her voice carrying the weight of her emotions like a melody echoing through the heart of the forest.

"Clusters of rose-apple trees, near the mere,
All the fruitage of the woods, my children are not here.
Fig tree and jack-fruit, banyan, every tree that grows,
All the fruitage of the woods, my children are not close.
They used to stand in a nice park where the river flows,

A place where they'd play, but now, my children are not close.

The fruit they used to eat, the flowers they used to wear,
Upon the hill, they once roamed, but my children are not there.

Little toys they used to play with, oxen, horses, elephants,
All those memories linger, but my children are absent.

Hares, owls, dark and spotted deer once played so near,
Peacocks with their gorgeous wings, herons, and geese now disappear.

With these creatures, they'd play in a world so dear,
But now, my children, where are you? Not close, not here."

Yet, despite her every effort, her cries were met with a resounding silence, a symphony of absence that seemed to stretch to eternity. Maddi's heart, aching and heavy, bore the weight of a love that yearned to bridge the chasm between longing and reality.

And still, the vacuum of words persisted, leaving her to navigate the tangle of uncertainty alone. With the moon casting its ethereal glow upon her, Maddi embarked on her quest, her heart a compass guiding her through the familiar corners of their world. The terrain, once etched with the indelible footprints of childhood revelry, now seemed to echo the emptiness of their absence.

***

Amidst the tapestry of nature's wonder, as the tender light of dawn washed over the verdant landscape, Maddi's heart remained a canvas painted with the hues of worry and sorrow. The once serene hermitage now held an air of emptiness, its silence punctuated only by the mournful rustling of leaves. With each step, Maddi's gaze flitted like a butterfly among the flowering plants, seeking her cherished children, Jali and Kanhajina.

"Within these woods, where blossoms paint the very air with their hues, where laughter used to dance like sunlight on leaves, there's naught but a lingering echo of their presence," she lamented, her voice weaving a delicate tapestry of longing. The tranquil lakes, whose ripples had once embraced their joyous giggles, now stood as silent witnesses to the void left in their wake. "Lotus blooms, white and blue, stand sentinel like sentries guarding an emptiness," she mused, her words echoing the heartache of a mother's longing.

Yet, despite her earnest quest, the woods offered no solace. Like notes of a sad melody, her footsteps led her back to the Great Being, his head bowed as if contemplating secrets known only to him. Her voice, a river of concern, flowed forth once more. "The hearth remains untouched, its flames unkindled. The water fetcher's task, undertaken with love and devotion, remains untouched. What weighs upon your thoughts, O noble man? Why this stillness, this unsettling calm?"

Her plea, like a fragile bird taking flight, hung in the air. "As I return to the refuge of our humble abode, the absence of Jali and Kanhajina appears like a shadow," she sighed. "Where could they be, my heart's delight, lost in the tangled woods of uncertainty?"

The air seemed heavy with unanswered questions, the space between them echoing her disquiet. Still, the

Great Being remained cloaked in silence, a silence that gnawed at her like a persistent ache. Resolute, Maddi ventured forth again, her heart fluttering like a leaf caught in a breeze. As if guided by an invisible thread, she retraced her steps, searching the familiar haunts that had once echoed with her children's laughter.

Returning once more to the presence of the Great Being, her voice a mixture of concern and an unspoken plea, she prayed, "My lord, my heart aches for your words. Is it my deeds that have caused this silence? Have I, unknowingly, strayed from the path we tread together?"

Like a fragile thread woven from the fabric of love, her voice unraveled in the face of his steadfast quietude. "As if a veil of silence has draped itself over our world, your words remain hidden," she whispered, her heart aching with the weight of unanswered questions.

With a determination as fierce as a storm, Maddi embarked on a third search, her steps carrying her across hills and valleys through forests that whispered secrets only the wind could decipher. As the night aged, she journeyed fifteen leagues, driven by a desperation that mirrored the frantic flutter of a caged bird.

As dawn's gentle fingers brushed the sky, Maddi stood once more before the Great Being, her form a portrait of determination tinged with sorrow. "Through woods and hills, caves and open glades, I have searched," she spoke, her voice a weary cadence of longing. "But even under the watchful eyes of the ravens, no sign of them remains."

In the depths of the forest, beneath the canopy of ancient trees, Maddi, a lady of noble lineage, found herself surrendering to the waves of sorrow that crashed against the shores of her heart. Her regal spirit, once as luminous as the morning sun on dew-kissed petals, was now dimmed by the weight of her anguish. Her arms stretched out in a gesture of supplication, her cries of lamentation echoing through the stillness of the woods.

The Great Being Vessantara watched her from a distance, his heart a battleground of conflicting emotions. Fear overtook him as he saw her lying down, imagining the worst. "She cannot pass away here," he thought with a shudder, "not in the quiet shadows of this forest. Her passing should be a grand event, reverberating through the halls of Jetuttara city, causing kingdoms to stir."

His mind was a whirlwind of thoughts, his distress threatening to consume him. He knew he needed to act, to find a way to revive her, to pull her back from the precipice of her grief.

With resolve, he approached her, his steps cautious as if treading on sacred ground. He placed a trembling hand on her chest, feeling for the faint stirrings of life within. Then, with urgency, he fetched water, his ascetic principles momentarily forgotten in the face of his deep concern. As her head rested on his lap, he gently sprinkled water on her, his touch as tender as a whisper in the wind. His fingers traced the contours of her face, his touch a balm to her wounded spirit.

Maddi's eyelashes fluttered like a butterfly emerging from its cocoon in the tranquil moments that followed. Awareness returned to her like a gentle dawn and, with it, a flood of questions. She greeted her husband with reverence, her voice laden with curiosity and a hint of reproach. "My Lord Vessantara, where are our children?" Her voice trembled with a mixture of hope and dread.

The Great Being Vessantara responded with a measured tone, calmly delivering the truth despite the storm within him. "I have given them," he replied, a statement that held worlds of complexity and emotion.

And so, he recounted the tale of his giving, explaining the circumstances that had led to this heart-wrenching decision. Maddi listened, her heart torn between the knowledge of his selfless act and the agony of separation from her beloved children.

"Why then," she questioned, her voice a mixture of vulnerability and frustration, "did you let me wander through the night, weeping and lost?"

His answer was laced with understanding, a confession of his fear for her heartache, a sentiment that transcended the limitations of words.

In response, Maddi's emotions rippled through her like a river in flood. Joy intermingled with pain, relief tangled with reproach. She understood his intentions and the depth of his sacrifice but couldn't help but question the path they were now on.

With a smile that held both tenderness and strength, the Great Being reassured her. "Maddi, let not your heart be burdened. In doing so, we shall reclaim them and embrace a greater gift – the gift of generous hearts."

Her reply was a powerful reflection of her determined and resilient character. Her articulate words expressed their shared beliefs and principles with great conviction. 'Absolutely,' she declared with unwavering confidence, 'let us welcome this opportunity to give yet again. Let us relish in the infinite happiness it brings.'

CHAPTER 9

THE ACCOUNT OF THE KING SAKKA

In the heart of the hermitage, where shadows whispered ancient secrets, the Great Being Vessantara, immersed in the cloak of contemplation, offered no response to Maddi's moving lament. The night unfolded, adorned with the moon's silvery glow, casting a spectral luminescence over the sacred sanctuary.

Undeterred by the ominous silence that lingered like a shadow, Maddi, her heart aflutter with anxiety, embarked on a desperate search beneath the moon's watchful gaze. Every familiar nook and cranny that once cradled her children's laughter became a haunting ground for her tears. In trembling whispers, she voiced her anguish to the moonlit shadows.

The King of gods, Sakka, received an idea that could guide the paths of Vessantara and Maddi towards a higher level of virtue. He decided to disguise himself as a humble Brahmin and make a simple request for Maddi. He believed that this could help Vessantara's virtue shine ever brighter and elevate his spiritual journey. Sakka saw this as an opportunity not just to test Vessantara's resolve but also to restore the intricate tapestry of fate by reuniting Maddi with her husband once the purpose was fulfilled.

With the arrival of dawn, the celestial plan began to unfurl. Sakka, donning the appearance of a wandering Brahmin, set foot upon the forest path that led to Vessantara's dwelling. His unassuming and humble appearance concealed the boundless power that resided within.

Approaching Vessantara, the disguised Sakka greeted him with warmth:
"Good day, noble sir. I hope you're well and thriving,
With grains and fruits, in solitude, surviving.
Have insects and pests caused trouble, pray to tell,
Or wild beasts posed threats in this tranquil dell?"

Vessantara, the epitome of generosity and equanimity, responded with a gracious smile:
"I thank you, Brahmin, I am well and thriving,
With nature's bounty, I am still surviving.
No insects nor pests have brought me dismay,
And wild beasts have not crossed my path, I say.
Seven months in these woods, and it's pretty clear,
You're the second Brahmin to find me here."

Illustration 10: Disguised as a Brahmin, Indra, the king of gods, approaches Vessantara and requests his wife Maddi, to which Vessantara agrees.

In the gentle shade of the forest, Sakka's disguise became an unbroken veil, allowing him to blend effortlessly into Vessantara's world. The disguised celestial visitor was received with the same warmth that characterized Vessantara's hospitality towards all who came his way. He warmly welcomed the Brahmin, offering the fruits of the forest and cool water from a hidden cave. The hermitage enveloped in an air of mystique, bore witness to the unfolding drama that would test the virtuous King's resilience and illuminate the path to supreme perfection.

***

In the tranquil heart of the wooded sanctuary, Vessantara, the Great Being, engaged in a conversation with the enigmatic Brahmin. The air was thick with the scent of ancient trees, and the sounds of nature provided a symphony to their discourse.

Curiosity etched on the lines of his noble face, Vessantara queried the purpose behind the Brahmin's journey into the mighty woods. Sakka, wearing the guise of an old Brahmin, responded with a request that hung in the air like a delicate fragrance. "O King, I am old, but I have come here to beg your wife Maddi; pray give her to me," he entreated, framing his plea in verses that echoed like a distant melody.

The Great Being, unperturbed by the unusual request, stood in the midst of the forest's majesty. His countenance, a portrait of composure, bore witness to a mind untethered from worldly attachments. Yet, the echoes of a stanza reverberated through the ancient trees: "As a great water-flood is full and fails not any day, so you, from whom I come to beg—give me your wife, I pray."

In the profound silence that followed, Vessantara, guided by an unwavering inner calm, contemplated the intricate dance of fate. The weight of the decision rested on his shoulders, intertwined with the recent act of parting with his beloved children. Once a haven of solace, the forest seemed to hold its breath.

Without a word, he reached for a water jar, the King of Sivi land performing a ceremonial act that would seal the fate of Maddi. The water, a symbol of purity, cascaded over his hands, signifying the solemnity of the moment. Vessantara, the benevolent giver, handed Maddi over to the disguised Sakka in a gesture of unparalleled detachment.

As the exchange transpired, the woods bore witness to portents—nature's response to the unfolding cosmic drama. The very earth beneath them trembled, echoing the magnitude of the sacrifice.

"Then he took up a water jar, the King of Sivi land, and took Maddi and gave her straight into the Brahmin's hand. Then was there terror and affright, then the great earth did quake, What time he rendered Maddi for his visitor to take."

Maddi, in her silence, accepted the profound act with grace. The pageant of sacrifice unfolded—a sacrifice not born of hatred for the family but a devotion to perfect knowledge, a transcendence that elevated wisdom above personal bonds.

As Vessantara spoke:
"Both Jali and Kanhajina, I let another take,
And Maddi, my devoted wife, and all for wisdom's sake.
Not hateful is my faithful wife, nor yet my children are,
But perfect knowledge, to my mind, is something dearer far."

The forest whispered its assent, bearing witness to a sacrifice made in the crucible of wisdom, where love and detachment danced hand in hand.

With a shift of attention, the Great Being turned his gaze upon Maddi, his heart filled with a curious blend of anticipation and apprehension. In this pivotal moment, he sought to glimpse the depth of her emotions and the steadfastness of her resolve. Maddi, the epitome of unyielding determination, met his gaze with unflinching courage and spoke in a voice that resonated with strength:
"From maidenhood till now, his wife I've proudly stood,
Through commands, through fate's turns, whether bad or good.
To give or take, to sell or kill, my heart remains the same,
In loyalty and love, I bear your name."

Thus, Maddi declared, her words carrying a regal authority that echoed the resolute spirit within her.

Sakka, the celestial observer of this human event, couldn't help but be impressed by the resolute spirit that flowed from Maddi's words. Her declaration was a testament to the profound bond that transcended mere circumstance. He applauded her unyielding loyalty with words of praise:

"Obstacles you've conquered, your resolve is such.
Earth's heart did quake, its echoes reached the sky,
Thunder roared, and lightning flared up high.
Narada, Pabbata, and heavens above,
Rejoiced in this act of sacrifice and love.
Emulating virtue is no minor feat,
In paths of righteousness, many souls meet.
For wrongdoers, hell awaits in its embrace,
Heaven's reward crowns those who goodness chase.
This is the Noble Path, a radiant light,
With wife and child surrendered, embracing what's right.
May he never descend from this virtuous height,
May these noble acts lead to heavens so bright."

Sakka, content that his design had borne the desired fruit, acknowledged that it was time for Maddi to be returned to Vessantara. He spoke with a tone that carried the weight of fulfilled purpose:
"Sir, I return to you Maddi, your beloved spouse,
A bond that endures, weaving life's noble house.
Like water and its vessel in nature's grand plan,
You and Maddi, a match divinely planned.

Two families linked by fate, status held with pride,
In this forest sanctuary, love shall always reside.
May your deeds shine with virtue, wise and just,
In your leafy haven, a sanctuary of trust."

Sakka's benevolent intent was further unveiled as he extended an offer to Vessantara, a boon that mirrored the celestial scope of his presence:

"I am Sakka, King of the gods. Here I stand, choosing a boon, O royal sage, and granting a wish so grand. Eight desires I'll fulfill, dreams woven anew, name your heart's yearning, and I shall make it true."

Sakka's voice resonated, a celestial echo, as he lofted himself into the sky, akin to the morning sun ascending its throne. His departure left the earthly realm bathed in a sense of tranquil wonder. Standing in the forest's heart, Vessantara, a Great Being in both spirit and presence, poised himself to make a profound choice – a choice that would weave destiny's threads into an intricate tapestry of aspirations and blessings.

***

With a demeanor of unwavering calm, the Great Being Vessantara began to articulate his wishes, the utterance of each word resonating with a resonance that seemed to ripple through the fabric of existence itself:

"Sakka, sovereign of lands vast, offers boons that sway destiny's tide.

First, may my father's arms embrace me once more, A reunion of hearts, a bond to restore.

May I never decree a life's early end, even if the darkness in hearts may descend.

The people's burdens, let me shoulder with care, Guiding them through life's trials and fares.

May fidelity grace my wife's loving face, Lust's treacherous snares forever erased.

A son, my lineage's heir, a realm's destiny, A noble ruler, just and unwaveringly free.

Let dawn's light bear bounties to nourish all, Fear dispelled, sustenance at every hearth's call.
May the spirit of giving forever endure, A beacon of kindness, a joy pure.
Lastly, grant me the boundless sky, Where rebirth's cycle can but sigh."

Sakka, the divine listener, caught these words like ethereal notes, a smile illuminating his features as he responded with a celestial embrace of affirmation:
"In your father's heart, a longing will ignite,
Drawing you back from the distant flight."

And as his words kissed the air, Sakka took his leave, a return to his heavenly abode, leaving behind an earthly domain resonating with the potential of fulfilled destinies. The Great Being, ever rooted in virtue's soil, stood amidst the whispering leaves and rustling secrets, his thoughts the calm center of this cosmic whirlpool. And so, the threads of fate intertwined, and the prophecy of Sujampati, the sacred tale, began its journey to fulfillment, a testament of nobility and grace for all to behold.

CHAPTER 10

THE SEGMENT CONCERNING THE
GREAT KING

In the serene embrace of the hermitage granted by Sakka's benevolence, Vessantara and Maddi found solace. The woods whispered with tranquility as they built a life amid nature's nurturing grace. Their days were an ode to simplicity, as they tended to the garden of their souls and nurtured the bond that was the very essence of their existence. Laughter and whispers of love floated in the air, painting a portrait of happiness that could rival the heavens.

Meanwhile, Jujaka's journey stretched onward, a weary path that spanned sixty leagues of untamed wilderness. A shadow against nature's grandeur, he dragged the children along like burdens, their innocent laughter silenced by the gravity of his greed. As the sun dipped beneath the horizon, he bound them with osiers, a cruel reminder of their captivity. Yet, under the watchful gaze of benevolent deities, no harm befell them.

Fearful of the forest's nocturnal residents, Jujaka would take refuge amidst the sheltering branches of a tree, the safety of its embrace his only sanctuary. Yet, divine figures took form in a realm beyond mortal sight – the embodiment of Vessantara and Maddi's compassion. Approaching the children, they gently loosened the binds that imprisoned their tiny forms. They tended to the children's needs with celestial tenderness, filling their world with comfort, care, nourishment, and a respite of ethereal dreams.

As the night's embrace yielded to the embrace of dawn, the deities would carefully tuck the children back into their bonds, their presence fading into the unseen tapestry of existence. Guided by these celestial hands, the children's journey remained untouched by the darkness that could have befallen them.

Meanwhile, divine threads continued to weave the tale, their influence extending even to the kingdom of Sivi. King Sanjaya's dreams bore the mark of fate's hand, heralding the return of those long absent. Intrigued by the visions of the night, he sought counsel from his wise Brahmins. Their voices, a melody of prophecy, unveiled the significance of the dream – a harbinger of the homecoming of warriors who had long graced foreign lands.

Illustration 11: Disguised as Vessantara and Maddi, the celestial gods care for Kanhajina and Jali while Jujaka sleeps deeply in a hammock.

Following their counsel, the kingdom stirred with grandeur as a feast worthy of legends was set in motion, and the royal court became a tapestry of vibrant colors and regal splendor. In this resplendence, the deities played their part, guiding Jujaka to the palace's very heart.

As Jujaka appeared before the assembled nobility, his captives by his side, the King's eyes fell upon the children – radiant souls akin to sun-kissed gold. His voice resonated with wonder as he spoke:
"Whose faces shine like molten gold, kissed by the sun's warm light,
Ardent and luminous, as if fire breathed upon them each night?
Bound by resemblance, two blossoms of youth they bear,
A striking likeness to Jali and Kanhajina, a pair.
Lion-hearted cubs emerging from a hidden den,
Treasures aglow in golden hues, radiant amidst the glen."

In the resplendent court of Sivi, King Sanjaya's attention lingered on the radiant children who stood before him, their very presence akin to two blossoms freshly kissed by dawn's embrace. It was as if the sunlight itself danced upon their innocent faces. Praise flowed from the monarch's lips, flowing like a river of admiration sculpted by the hands of genuine delight. With a sweep of his hand, he beckoned a courtier to fetch them, and without ado, the children were ushered into the heart of the regal chamber.

Turning to the Brahmin, Bharadvaja, whose role in this intricate tapestry was now revealed, the King queried, his voice a reflection of his intrigue:

"Good Bharadvaja, from whence do these children hail?"

In response, Jujaka spoke with an air of casual indifference:

"O noble King, merely a fortnight past, these cherished children were placed in my care, a gift borne of someone's satisfaction with my humble request."

The King's curiosity deepened, his eyes reflecting a quiet intensity:

"Tell me, then, how did you manage to earn this precious bounty? How did you sway the heart of the bestower?"

Jujaka's lips curved into a sinister smile, his reply calculated:

"It was none other than Vessantara, who, amidst the wilderness, resides. His generosity, akin to the earth's boundless offerings, extended to granting his own offspring — a royal bestowment, gifted as if culled from the sea's inexhaustible depths."

The courtiers, a canvas of varied expressions, spoke aloud their disapproval, their words a collective chorus of judgment:

"Such an act, if spoken of the King's own lips, would seem beyond belief, yet you narrate it as reality. But tell us, is it possible that he parted with his progeny during his very exile, these treasures of his very soul?"

Amid this sea of skepticism, the boy's voice, clear as a mountain stream, cut through the murmur like a clarion call:

"What is there to give away if one does not truly own? Can a man relinquish what is not truly his – children, slaves, or even the mightiest of elephants?"

A solemn hush descended, a mere breath of silence enveloping the court. King Sanjaya's gaze, a study in contemplation, met the boy's unwavering stare. In his voice lay both conviction and respect: "Your words are a salve to my heart, a wisdom profound beyond your years. Yet, noble children, in my quest for truth, let me ask – what emotions graced your father's heart as he made this grand offering?"

The boy's reply, a portrait of raw emotion, painted the air with its vivid hues:

"Sorrow, like a consuming fire, danced within his eyes, his heart a pyre of burning pain. Tears, unbidden, streamed like Rohini's radiant trail, his sacrifice etched with a thousand unspoken words."

In the tranquil chambers of the royal palace, an unsettling conversation unfolded between the King, Sanjaya, and his two children, Kanhajina and Jali. The Brahmin, their apparent captor, was accused by Kanhajina of cruelty and deception.

"O King, this Brahmin treats us like slaves, wielding cruelty as his weapon. He defies the essence of his own title, masquerading as a goblin beneath the guise of a Brahmin's robe. How can you let him strip us of our dignity and bear such an ordeal? Should you not rise to defend us, your flesh and blood?"

The boy, her brother, stood in solidarity, reinforcing her claim against the Brahmin's legitimacy.

The narrative flowed like a river of fate, each word shaping destiny's course. Amid this tumultuous sea, the King's voice reclaimed center stage, reciting verses of kinship, each line an offering of love:
"Offspring of a royal line, descendants of a regal grace,
Once you perched upon my hips, now a distant stance you trace."

Yet, the boy's voice, fervent and unyielding, wove the next stanza into the tapestry:
"We, noble in lineage and birth, now slaves in deed,
Brahmin's cruelty shackles us, as if planted by a wicked seed."

In this poignant exchange, the very essence of their connection shined like a distant star, unwavering in the expanse of fate's canvas. King Sanjaya's voice, both determined and tender, rose in unison:
"Beloved children, cease your mournful cries,
Your words sting like a thousand arrows.
Let not this distance sever our bond,
For I stand ready to ransom your freedom,
A tribute to your rightful place, with love and pride."

Their voices a harmonious symphony, the sum agreed, the bond affirmed. The steward moved with a grace befitting the occasion, gifting the Brahmin with a bounty that mirrored the kingdom's grandeur. One hundred slaves, male and female, walked forth, their footsteps a tribute to the King's generosity. And a hundred elephants and bulls paraded in majestic splendor, a living testament to prosperity's touch.

But the grandeur did not cease here, for the King, a patron of opulence, granted the Brahmin a palace of seven stories.

Storing away his newfound treasures, the Brahmin ascended to his opulent palace, where intricately carved pillars and golden embellishments adorned each floor. Reclining on a sumptuous couch at the pinnacle of luxury, he indulged in a banquet of choice meats, the plush fabric cradling him as he savored the flavors.

***

Having been well-washed, dressed in opulence, and nourished, the Prince and the Princess were placed on their grandparents' hips. At that moment, King Sanjaya addressed Jali, expressing trust in the prosperity and well-being of her parents. He inquired whether their dwelling was abundant with grain to harvest and if roots and fruits flourished plentifully. The King sought to know if they had endured the nuisances of flies, gnats, and crawling creatures and if they had found immunity from the threat of wild beasts of prey.

The young lad respectfully addressed the King, offering his gratitude before revealing his parents' well-being.

"Thank you, noble King," Prince Jali began, "Allow me to share that my parents thrive. In their realm, the land yields an abundance of grain, roots, and fruits. They are spared the vexation of flies, gnats, and creeping creatures and enjoy immunity from the lurking threat of wild beasts. With unwavering dedication, my mother forages for wild bulbs, radishes, catmint, herbs, jujubes, nuts, and vilva fruit, ensuring a constant supply of sustenance. Whenever she returns with the harvest, be it wild fruits or roots, our family gathers to partake in the feast, both day and night."

The little Prince then shifted his narrative to the hardships his mother endured.

"However," he continued, his voice tinged with concern, "my mother has grown thin and pale in her quest for our sustenance. She navigates the beast-haunted wood, enduring the harsh elements—exposed to both heat and wind. Like a delicate lotus flower held in a fading hand, her hair, once lush, has thinned due to her wanderings in the forest glades. Clotted dirt gathers beneath her armpits, and her hair is tied in a simple topknot. Despite her hardships, she tends to the fire and sleeps upon the ground, clad in skins."

With a mixture of gratitude and reproach, Prince Jali confronted his grandfather.

"It is customary in the world for a father to love his son," he asserted, "Yet, in this particular instance, it appears that such an honor has been neglected."

King Sanjaya, admitting his faults, spoke with a voice heavy with remorse, which echoed through the

palace corridors and beyond, touching the hearts of all who heard his confession:
"In truth, a grievous error I did commit,
Innocence harmed, a son's fate unfit.
Led astray by voices clamoring near,
My decision unjust, my son's fate severe.
All the riches I've amassed, the kingdom I hold,
I offer to him, my repentance untold.
Let Vessantara rule, his virtues shine,
In Sivi's grandeur, his reign entwine."

As the words hung in the air, young Jali, wise beyond his years, stepped forward, his gaze steady and voice unwavering:
"Return he won't, to rule or command,
If his presence you seek, go yourself, take a stand."

King Sanjaya turned, his resolve crystallized, and addressed his loyal chief general:
"Ready my horses, the chariots arrayed,
Elephants are majestic, by loyalty, swayed.
Summon the masses, the priests, and the wise,
Gather the realm and let unity rise.

Sixty thousand warriors, valiant and grand,
Arrayed in armor, a noble band.
Hues of blue, brown, and white they don,
With crests agleam, like the morning sun.

Their spirits high, their hearts aligned,
As victory's song, the winds shall wind.
Then, fourteen thousand elephants tall,
In gold-adorned splendor, an awe-inspiring call.

A nimble array, skilled drivers at hand,
Guiding with lance and hook, their stance so grand.
Chariots fourteen thousand, a sight to behold,
Crafted with skill, adorned in gold.

Iron-wheeled marvels and banners unfold,
Shields of might, inlaid with stories untold.
Archers ready, their aim held tight,
Warriors brave, their resolve a radiant light."

Thus, the King commanded his formidable army's formation, his orders echoing like a clarion call throughout the kingdom.

***

With a determination that echoed in the very stones of the royal road, the path from Jetuttara to Mount Vamka was meticulously prepared. The air was saturated with the fragrance of Laja flowers, scattered like morning dew along the route. Garlands of reverence adorned the path, paying homage to the significance of the impending journey.

From every village, a hundred jars of wine were poured, a collective gesture of welcome that felt like a divine passage. Meats, cakes, and fish-filled broth were laid along the path, creating a feast on the ground for the travelers. The offerings spoke of abundance and hospitality, each dish a testament to the devotion that underscored the preparations.

Wine, oil, ghee, milk, rice, and curds, pure and untainted, stood as offerings, symbolizing the wealth of the land and the sincerity of the people's devotion. A lively brigade of cooks and bakers worked tirelessly, ensuring that each morsel carried not just sustenance but a piece of their collective spirit.

In the midst of this bustling preparation, musicians and dancers formed a jubilant parade. Lutes and conches echoed through the air, accompanied by the rhythmic sound of drums, tabours, and timbrels. Joy seemed unbound as if the very fabric of the atmosphere vibrated with the anticipation of the impending journey.

"May this tapestry of offerings pave the way for redemption and reunion," the King intoned, his voice resonating with a mixture of solemnity and hope. His gaze lingered on the preparations, appreciating the dedication that went into crafting this intricate display of devotion.

As they navigated through this intricate backdrop, their unique personalities became more apparent. King Sanjaya, a figure of redemption, bore the weight of past decisions, his determination a shield against the shadows of regret. The cooks and bakers, the often overlooked heroes of this culinary ensemble, displayed a commitment to their craft that mirrored the devotion of the people.

Thus, the preparations unfolded like an intricate tapestry, woven with care and devotion, as the King readied himself to embark on a journey of redemption and reunion.

***

While the kingdom bustled with activity, Brahmin Jujaka found solace in the luxurious feasts and comforts bestowed upon him by the King. Jujaka's voracious indulgence proved his undoing, for his gluttony led him to an untimely demise. Yet, in death, as in life, he remained alone, his ties severed, and his worldly possessions returned to the King.

On the seventh day, the realm assembled, converging in a manifestation of solidarity rarely witnessed. The city square transformed into a mosaic of vibrant life, echoing the heartbeat of a kingdom on the cusp of destiny. At the forefront of this grand assembly stood the King, draped in regal attire that bespoke both authority and vulnerability. His gaze, a mixture of solemnity and unwavering determination, surveyed the multitude that had come to witness a pivotal juncture in the kingdom's saga.

***

In the realm of Jetuttara, the royal road to Mount Vamka unfurled with unwavering determination. Young Jali stood at the forefront of this grand expedition, a living emblem of undying devotion. Though tender in years, Jali emanated a quiet strength, a testament to the resilience instilled by the trials weathered alongside his sister, Kanhajina.

The march of grandeur took shape like a majestic dance, an army vast and purposeful, their destiny a palpable force propelling them forward. With each step measured, a mighty force surged with the commitment to fulfill their mast.

Amidst the procession, a sixty-year-old elephant, a living monument of strength, rumbled with echoes that served as a proclamation of their intent. Chariots creaked, horses neighed, and a harmonious symphony enveloped them, aligning their collective purpose in a rhythmic cadence.

The warriors, embodiments of preparedness, stood armed and equipped, their readiness palpable in the air. Jali, the youthful guide with wisdom beyond his years, fearlessly charted the path ahead, undeterred by the uncertainties that loomed.

As they ventured into the expansive and green forest, an untouched sanctuary unfolded, where nature's serenity was at its purest. Blossoming flowers and lush fruits adorned this wild heart, a testament to the inherent beauty concealed within.

The odyssey unfolded seamlessly, day and night, melding into a rhythmic journey. Unwavering determination and decree propelled them through winding trails and undulating land, each step a testament to their unwavering devotion.

Within this expedition, they encountered a sanctuary of blooming beauty meticulously crafted by the hand of life. This sanctuary marked the gateway to the realm where Vessantara's virtues radiated with a brilliant glow.

CHAPTER 11

THE SIX VIRTUOUS WARRIORS

Prince Jali orchestrated the establishment of a camp near the tranquil shores of Lake Mucalinda. The shores of Mucalinda sprawled beneath a vast canvas of boundless sky, a sanctuary where nature unfolded its finest tapestry. The lake, a serene expanse of crystal-clear water, mirrored the heavens above, creating an ethereal connection between earth and sky.

With meticulous precision, the procession of fourteen thousand chariots stood sentinel, their formidable presence aligned to face the road whence they had journeyed. Guards, vigilant and resolute, stationed themselves at strategic intervals, their eyes trained on the surrounding wilderness, wary of the beasts that stalked through the underbrush. The atmosphere was filled with a harmonious symphony - the resonating trumpets of elephants, the rhythmic drumming of hooves, and the firm proclamation of authority.

Amidst this orchestrated overture of sound, the Great Being Vessantara's heart stirred with an uneasy trepidation. Could it be that harm had befallen his father, and now those very forces approached, intent on capturing him? Clasping Maddi's hand, a lifeline of comfort, Vessantara ascended a nearby hill. His eyes scanned the horizon, where the impending grandeur of the approaching army came into view.

In a voice both pensive and foreboding, he voiced his thoughts: "Maddi, do you hear the cacophony that permeates the woods? The neighing steeds, the resolute drums, it's a symphony of goods. Could it be hunters brandishing snares and traps with guile, seeking to ensnare the innocent in a wretched, cruel trial? In this heart of the wild, exiled and misunderstood, do we now face the encroaching peril of a hostile neighborhood?"

Maddi, her gaze unwaveringly fixed on the oncoming procession, responded with soothing reassurance, her words flowing like a soothing balm to his fears:
"Fear not, my love, for enemies' plots are futile, you see,
Just as the fierce fire succumbs to the boundless sea."

Her voice carried conviction, a beacon of solace that eased his anxiety. He found the anchor to his fears in her gaze, a sanctuary against the storm. Empowered by her steadfastness, Vessantara descended the hillside, their entwined hands a testament to their unwavering unity. They settled before the haven of their leafy abode, their presence a testament to the resilience of the human spirit in the face of uncertainty.

***

King Sanjaya summoned his Queen, Phusati, his heart heavy with the weight of anticipation and uncertainty. His voice, soft yet resolute, carried his thoughts to her: "Phusati, my beloved, hear my words, I pray, Together, our presence might overwhelm them today. Let me venture forth alone to pave the way; once serenity reigns, you and the retinue can join without delay."

As time unfurled its steady march, King Sanjaya's thoughtful plan materialized. Prince Jali and Princess Kanhajina, summoned by the royal summons, stood by their grandfather's side. His chariot, a symbol of his station, pivoted to face the very road from which he had emerged, each detail a testament to his purpose. The strategic placement of vigilant guards reinforced his determination, a silent promise that no harm would befall his beloved son.

Upon a resplendent elephant adorned in regal attire, the King commenced his journey, the very fabric of his robe a tribute to both royalty and humility. His hands, raised in a prayerful gesture, resonated with a sincere hope, a father's aspiration to reclaim his kin. As the dense foliage of the forest enveloped him, Sanjaya pressed forward, an amalgamation of King and father, ruler and supplicant, his heart entwined with love and responsibility.

***

There, amidst the embrace of nature's grandeur, Vessantara and Maddi, a bastion of tranquility, sensed the approach of a presence familiar yet estranged. With a serene aura, Vessantara, composed and unshaken, continued his meditative reverie, a testament to his unwavering resilience. The anticipation lingered until the moment when their world shifted. Father and son, reunited by destiny's intricate design, found themselves on converging paths.

Maddi, her demeanor a blend of grace and humility, paid homage to her father-in-law, her head bowing in deference to his station. The embrace that followed spoke volumes, a silent exchange of understanding and acceptance, a bridge spanning the chasm of time and circumstance. Thus, amidst the embrace of nature's timeless beauty, the ties that bound them were reaffirmed, their unity an affirmation of their shared bloodline.

With a voice that trembled with a mixture of emotions, the King's words echoed through the air, a heartfelt inquiry that hung in the balance: "My son, I hope these woods have cradled you with care; amidst nature's bounty, its grains, fruits, and offerings are rare. Were the buzzing insects a vexation to your peace, or did the wild brethren of the woods find their release?"

The Great Being Vessantara addressed his father with a voice that resonated with the echoes of resilience forged through trials. The timbre of his words bore the weight of years spent navigating the harshness of their chosen existence: "Father, the path we've trodden has been arduous, our existence a symphony of endurance.

We've faced adversity with unyielding determination, akin to a charioteer mastering a spirited steed. These challenges, though daunting, have molded us into steadfast souls. But, it's the aching void left by our parents' absence that has cast the deepest shadow upon our well-being. Cast out from the realm we called home, thrust into the embrace of these wild woods and untamed forests, our frames have withered with the weight of time."

A furrow formed on his brow as his gaze pierced the King, a father yearning for news of his own progeny: "Yet, my heart is heavy with concern for my own offspring, Jali and Kanhajina. Those innocent souls, ensnared in the grip of a remorseless Brahmin, reduced to a status less than that of cattle. Father, do you bear tidings of them? Pray, share it as a healer might tend to a soul poisoned by the fangs of a serpent."

The King's response, spoken with a tone of assurance, carried the warmth of a father soothing his child's anxieties: "Jali and Kanhajina, your cherished lineage, have been delivered from the clutches of that Brahmin's grasp. I have paid the price demanded, releasing them from their ordeal. Fear not, my son, for they are safe."

A sigh of relief lifted from the Great Being's chest, and a cascade of emotions surged through him. This familial reunion, an intimate dance of hearts reuniting after the relentless trials of fate, unfurled like the tender petals of a blossoming lotus.

"My father, I pray your health has remained steadfast and that adversities have relinquished their grip. And may my mother's eyes find respite from the ceaseless torrents of sorrow."

The King's visage, graced with the soft curvature of a father's smile, mirrored the depths of their shared bond: "Thank you, my dear son. My well-being stands unblemished, and tribulations have been stilled. As for your mother, tranquility has claimed her heart and the curtain of endless tears no longer veils her eyes."

Within this rhythm of shared wishes and exchanged emotions, the Great Being extended his hopes like petals unfurling in the embrace of dawn: "May the kingdom flourish under its rule, may the lands find serenity in their embrace, and may the creatures of the wild bear their burdens with resilience. May the benevolent clouds continue their life-giving dance, gracing the earth with their blessings."

The King's words, a reflection of the monarch's heart, resonated harmoniously: "Indeed, the kingdom prospers under the canopy of your rule, tranquility sways through the landscapes, and our loyal companions of the wild bear their responsibilities with vigor. In their benevolence, the skies themselves bestow their blessings upon our realm."

As this symphony of conversations entwined, the forest clearing became a stage for the reunion of not just father and son but of a family's love that had traversed the crucible of trials and emerged unscathed.

***

"Amidst the rustling leaves and the whispering breeze, the verdant clearing welcomed the graceful figure of Queen Phusati. With each step, she exuded an air of regal authority softened by maternal affection. Vessantara and Maddi, embodying both reverence and sheer joy, rose to greet her, their gestures a symphony of respect and love. Maddi, touched by a wave of emotion, knelt humbly, her head bowing in profound adoration at the feet of her revered mother-in-law. It was a moment that beautifully captured the bond of generations, the intertwining threads of tradition and love."

As Phusati's gaze swept over her children, her heart swelled with an overwhelming mixture of relief and emotion:

"Maddi's eyes shimmered like pools of liquid emotion, her joy and relief mingling in silent tears as she beheld her children before her. They stood sturdy and unharmed, reminiscent of young calves under the watchful gaze of their mother cow. The air was filled with the palpable tenderness of their reunion, their voices a harmonious echo that resounded through the tranquil woods."

And amidst this tapestry of emotions, as conversations merged into a chorus of shared sentiments, Maddi's heart seemed to surge, the very essence of her being aflame with love and relief:

Illustration 12: The six members of the virtuous royal family reunite, marking a joyous and emotional moment of reunion.

"Maddi's heart raced like the swift current of a river, a torrent of emotions rushing through her veins as she beheld her children safe and sound. Her steps quickened, a yearning akin to a mother's protective instinct propelling her forward. Her eyes shimmered with unshed tears, her hands trembling with a potent mixture of joy and longing. At that moment, she felt as if her very core was filled with a nurturing warmth, much like the surging of milk-laden breasts nurturing the young."

A sudden silence fell upon the landscape as if nature was holding its breath in anticipation. The undulating hills, once silent witnesses to the unfolding play, now echoed with a resounding boom that seemed to reverberate through the very marrow of the earth. The ground trembled beneath their feet, a rhythmic dance of soil and stone swaying like the heartbeat of a slumbering giant. Even the vast expanse of the ocean appeared to shudder, its waves leaping and crashing against the shore in an agitated ballet. And then, in a gesture of awe-inspiring reverence, Sineru, the towering mountain that scraped the heavens, appeared to bow its majestic head in deference to an unseen force. It was as if the very earth and sky were paying homage to an unfathomable power.

***

Amidst this symphony of natural wonders, the celestial realms themselves seemed to converge in harmonious unity. The heavens blazed with an ethereal luminescence as if the stars and planets had aligned in a cosmic dance. The air hummed with an electric energy, a palpable vibration that set every nerve on edge. The six realms of the gods, usually distinct and separate, now resonated in a breathtaking symphony of convergence.

Amid this cosmic orchestration, Sakka, the illustrious ruler of the divine realms, beheld a sight of profound significance. Before him lay six figures, regal and motionless, caught in the thrall of an enchantment that seemed to transcend human understanding. Their entourages, frozen in time, surrounded them like loyal sentinels guarding a slumbering dynasty. Yet, they were helpless, unable to rise from their earthly beds or extend a comforting hand to one another. This surreal display spoke of a power beyond comprehension, a force that held even the mightiest in its thrall.

Determination ignited within Sakka's heart, the resolute flame of a guardian compelled to intervene. With a sweeping gesture that seemed to command the very heavens, he summoned a celestial rain shower. Droplets, glistening like liquid diamonds, descended from the expanse above. They fell with a gentle grace, a balletic descent that painted the air with a symphony of sound. Yet, this was no ordinary rain; it bore the essence of the divine, responding to the desires and intentions of those upon whom it bestowed its blessings.

As the rain kissed the earth, a miracle unfolded. Those who welcomed its touch felt its invigorating embrace, their forms drenched in its life-giving essence. It was a caress that awakened the senses, a reminder of nature's benevolence. Yet, for those who willed themselves to remain untouched, not a single droplet dared to breach their sanctuary. The rain seemed to cascade off them, a testament to their unyielding resolve, like water on the resilient surface of a lotus leaf.

This celestial downpour, a spectacle of divine artistry, resembled the gentle cascade that graces a bed of lotus blooms. And as the magical raindrops made contact with the six figures lying dormant, a transmutation occurred. Gradually, the mists of enchantment lifted like the parting of a curtain, and their senses began to stir. The onlookers, enthralled witnesses to this otherworldly drama, watched in rapt attention as the figures began to stir from their slumber.

As consciousness returned, the bonds of kinship reignited with an almost palpable ferocity. The King, the Queen, the son, the daughter-in-law, and the grandchildren—all found themselves together in a tapestry woven by fate. It was a moment suspended in time, an embrace of unity and love that transcended the trials of the past. The very air seemed to hum with an electric current of emotion as the heart's joy manifested physically, causing the hair on the nape to stand on end. Overwhelmed by the magnitude of the moment, the witnesses found their voices melding in a harmonious chorus of praise.

Tears flowed freely, their emotions cascading like the rain that had heralded this profound transformation. And as the echoes of awe subsided, the people, moved by a collective surge of reverence, extended their hands in both applause and supplication. Their voices, raised in earnest harmony, became a chorus of fervent entreaties, a plea that resonated with hope and longing.

Thus, in the heart of nature's grand theater, surrounded by hills that whispered secrets and oceans that murmured tales, Vessantara and Maddi stood as the embodiment of unity and leadership. Their subjects, gathered like eager spectators, their hearts alight with aspiration, implored with fervor: "Be our guides, our sovereigns, our compass through the shifting tides of existence. Let your rule breathe prosperity into our land, and in this juncture of unity and strength, lead us, O Vessantara and Maddi, to a future painted in the hues of your benevolence."

CHAPTER 12

VESSANTARA'S RETURN

The Great Being Vessantara stood before his father, his eyes reflecting his intense emotions. A heavy silence hung between them, laden with the unspoken words of a kingdom's betrayal. Finally, he spoke, his every word chosen with the utmost care, imbued with the weighty truth of his words.

"Dear father, both the villagers and city dwellers have cast me aside, a ruler ousted from his throne despite the righteousness and nobility that supported my reign."

His father's countenance bore the weight of his transgressions, remorse etched in the furrowed lines of his brow. With a voice heavy with repentance, he sought to mend the fragile strands of their bond.

"I stand shrouded in the shadows of regret, for my deeds have birthed your suffering, an agony I did not foresee, driven by the clamor of voices that were not my own."

The Great Being's eyes shimmered with an intricate tapestry of emotions as he acknowledged the wounds that had festered within him.

"To ease the ache that gnaws another's heart, be it the beat of a father's pulse, the tendrils of a mother's love, the companionship of a sister, or the embrace of a friend, one should never falter, even if the toll demanded is one's very life."

In the recesses of his soul, the Great Being Vessantara had harbored a wish, a yearning to reclaim the mantle of his rightful throne. Yet, with a masterful restraint that commanded respect, he chose to keep these thoughts veiled, allowing the chambers of silence to speak volumes.

Around him, a sea of sixty thousand courtiers, each a strand in the intricate tapestry of his lineage, swayed like eager leaves in the wind, their voices rising in an enthusiastic crescendo, "The time is ripe, mighty King, to cast away the veil that cloaks your grandeur, to rinse away the layers of dust and grime that time has woven."

However, the Great Being, with a serene gesture that seemed to quell the very air, murmured, "Patience, I beseech you." With measured steps, he withdrew into the sanctum of his modest abode, where the whispering leaves of solitude and contemplation embraced him.

There, he divested himself of the simple garb of an ascetic; each fold bearing witness to his time in the wilderness. In its stead, he adorned himself in the regal vestments that spoke of a lineage steeped in history, a heritage intertwined with the annals of kings.

Emerging from his solitude, he stood before them once more, a figure transformed, his bearing a testament to the harmonious marriage of dignity and humility. The stillness of the moment was pierced by the cadence of his voice, resonant and sure, declaring to the heavens and the earth, "Here, amidst these woods and within the heart of ascetic solitude, for nine months and beyond, I trod the paths of self-discipline, shaping my spirit, honing my art of giving until the very earth beneath quivered in acknowledgment."

With measured reverence, he circumambulated his humble abode thrice, a ritual of homage that spoke of gratitude interwoven with the fabric of existence itself. Bowing low, he touched his forehead to the ground in a fivefold prostration - a gesture that conveyed both humility and proclamation.

His attendants, with care as delicate as the touch of a breeze upon a petal, tended to his hair and beard, anointing his being with the sanctified water of ceremony. With each reverent touch, he seemed to blossom into an embodiment of regal majesty, a mirror reflecting the splendor of divinity's sovereignty.

In the hushed symphony of the universe, it was as if the cosmos itself whispered a decree, a proclamation that echoed across the tapestry of existence, "Thus did

Vessantara, the embodiment of benevolence and sacrifice, shed the mortal veil that cloaked him, emerging resplendent, a beacon of nobility cleansed from the dust and grime of trials endured."

The sun hung low in the sky, a celestial jewel casting its amber hues upon the landscape. Amidst this ethereal glow, the figure of the Great Being stood, a luminous beacon that seemed to gather the very radiance of the heavens. As his gaze traversed the world below, the very earth quivered as if stirred by the weight of his presence. Around him, a chorus of voices rose, words of benediction and reverence woven into eloquent verses that flowed like honeyed nectar from the lips of those who encircled him. Their words, like fragrant petals carried by the wind, swathed him in a tapestry of blessings.

A symphony of music swelled in the air, a symphony where each instrument sang a melodious ode to this momentous juncture. From the rhythmic beat of the drums to the lilting notes of the flute, the very atmosphere vibrated with a harmonious resonance. Even across the vast expanse of the ocean, a symphony akin to the roll of thunder reverberated as if nature itself joined in this grand orchestration.

Amidst this opulent tableau, a grand and adorned elephant, a living embodiment of majesty, was led forth. With a grace that belied its size, the elephant's eyes held a regal wisdom, and its gait exuded an air of tranquil strength. A priceless sword found its place around the Great Being's waist, a gleaming sentinel that bore testament to his courage and nobility. With a fluid motion that spoke of years of familiarity, he mounted the majestic creature, the symbiosis of man and beast, a testimony to a profound connection.

In a splendid circle around him stood his sixty thousand fellow courtiers, his birth companions, each a luminary in his own right, bedecked in attire that shimmered like stardust. Their collective presence was a living constellation, a reflection of his lineage's enduring grandeur.

Not far from this tableau, Maddi herself was enveloped in a ritual of purification and adornment. The consecrated water cascaded over her form, a cascade of liquid prayers that sanctified her being. As the droplets kissed her skin, voices rose in harmonious unison, invoking blessings that carried the weight of centuries.

"May Vessantara, your steadfast protector, watch over you," they intoned, their voices an invocation of guardianship, a shield woven from love and devotion. Each word, imbued with the enthusiasm of faith, seemed to infuse the very air with a sense of auspiciousness.

As the final droplets of consecrated water fell, a sense of renewal seemed to infuse the atmosphere. The scene, a tableau of resplendence and devotion, unfolded thus:
"His hair, pure as moonbeams, cascades in graceful waves,
Robes of regal resplendence adorn him, a King who bravely saves.
On the noble elephant, a partner fierce and fair,

Sixty thousand strong, birth companions rare.

Beside tranquil waters, Maddi stands, a vision to behold,

Cloaked in silken splendor, stories yet untold.

Voices of women, a melodic prayer in the air,

'Vessantara and Sanjaya, love and protection share!'

In this symphony of unity, past trials distant memories,

Within the serene realm, joyous and persistent melodies.

Emerging from ordeal, reborn as dawn's rays,

Great Being and beloved, life's wondrous journey ablaze.

Through the crucible of time, their story's drawn,

A saga of healing, love reborn.

In the tapestry of life, threads now spun,

A melody of joy, a journey begun.

In unity's embrace, memories distant,

Their love, a symphony, ever insistent.

The Great Being and his beloved, bound forever,

On a path of healing, they endeavor."

***

Joy danced in the Queen's eyes as she turned to her children, her voice carrying the weight of a mother's devotion and a sovereign's blessings.

"In the shadow of the forest's embrace, I abided, my bed the earth's gentle cradle, A vow held, a sacrifice made, for you, my children, my resolve unswayable.

Now, with that sacred oath fulfilled, I beseech the cosmos anew, May the virtues woven into our every act, a shield of protection construe. In mighty King Sanjaya's vigilant care, find sanctuary and virtue imbue.

Let your steps be guided by your father's legacy, my radiant light, His wisdom and compassion, like stars in the night, forever bright.

And to you, my dear daughter-in-law, I extend a mother's embrace, Wear these robes and ornaments, a symbol of our connection's grace."

With a tender touch, she gathered these gifts, delicately placing them in boxes as a manifestation of her enduring love:

"Silk and linen, soft as whispers, a mother-in-law's tender hand,

Enrobed Maddi's form, a celestial vision, a beauty that would withstand.

Necklaces that shimmered like moonlight, bangles with melodies to chime,

A headpiece adorned with dreams, and a jeweled belt, a sign of the sublime.

Each jewel, a fragment of affection, bestowed with heartfelt care,

Sent by a mother-in-law's devotion, they adorned her, a radiance rare.

In those treasures, Maddi stood, adorned like a goddess of old,

Her beauty, a canvas of cosmic hues, a tale of love and legends told.

As Cittalata's breeze caresses the swaying plantain with grace,

So did Maddi, robed and adorned, a vision of elegance, her beauty's embrace.

Graceful as a bird with vibrant plumes that paints the skies,

Her presence, a bewitching song, in every glance and guise.

An elephant, regal and robust, approached with
measured might,
Tusks reaching for the heavens, its aura a majestic sight.
Upon this noble creature, Maddi ascended, resolute and
serene,
No spear's threat or battle's roar could ruffle this regal
scene.
In grandeur, they ventured to the royal camp, a union of
majesty and grace,
King Sanjaya's vast assembly embraced the wilderness, a
jubilant embrace.
Under the Great Being's radiant aura, for a month's
blissful span,
The forest's creatures thrived, their harmonious chorus
a testament grand.
Within this sanctuary of life, where predator and prey
shared the bough,
A realm untouched by harm, bound by the sovereign vow.
And as their departure loomed, a harmonious sigh in
the air,
Birds, beasts, and all in nature's care whispered their
farewell, a moment rare."

After a month of jubilant festivities that painted the
forest with merriment, King Sanjaya, the wise monarch,
beckoned his chief commander. His voice carried the
weight of anticipation as he inquired, his eyes reflecting
both authority and fatherly concern.

"We've reveled in this haven of wilderness, embraced
nature's tranquil call,

Yet now, dear commander, tell me true, is the path prepared for my son's return, for the grand procession of all?"

With a salute and a heart brimming with loyalty, the commander replied, "Indeed, my lord, the path is paved; the route is set for this destined quest." He carried out his sovereign's will, sending a messenger to the woods, where Vessantara had found his rest.

And so, with a grand assembly of warriors and a sea of banners fluttering in the breeze, the royal parade embarked, a sight to behold, through valleys and forests, across hills and flowing leas.

***

On the horizon, the road stretched out like a regal tapestry, its surface adorned with petals and pennants swaying in the gentle breeze. The forest's edge whispered tales of the Prince Vessantara's recent presence, and the path unfurled towards Jetuttara's gates, weaving a narrative of anticipation and destiny.

Prince Jali, a figure of grace and purpose, led the procession of sixty thousand steadfast comrades. Their march resonated with valor, a chorus of loyalty and pride echoing through the air. Children and kin accompanied them, adding a touch of familial warmth to the grand spectacle.

Within this diverse tapestry were Brahmins and traders, united in the jubilant stride toward Jetuttara. The air carried a symphony of hopes, each step a confiding note in the collective melody of the journey.

Illustration 13:Vessantara receives a warm welcome in the city of Jetuttara

The procession was not merely a physical movement but a shared pilgrimage bound by dreams and aspirations. As they moved forward, each step resonated with the heartbeat of their shared dreams, turning the procession into a symphony of aspirations, echoing the collective hope of the virtuous royal family.

Noble elephants, their presence grand and commanding, trod with grace, guided by the gentle hands of mahouts. Chariots and men, an assembly bold and grand, traversed the land with a sense of purpose and unity.

The procession set forth with the royal guards alongside them, who were determined to fulfill their oath of protection. The sight was breathtaking, a manifestation of unity unfolding from the embrace of the hill to the worth of the city. Conversations hummed in the air, voices interweaving like threads in the rich tapestry of the journey.

The personalities of the characters emerged more vividly against this detailed backdrop. The Prince, stoic yet determined, bore the weight of leadership with grace. Comrades displayed varied personalities – some exuding bravado, others emanating quiet strength. The children brought an innocent joy that contrasted with the seasoned pride of the elders.

As they progressed, the setting evolved, revealing the landscapes through which they passed – the forest, the bustling city, and the welcoming gates of Jetuttara.

Emotions were palpable, the air filled with excitement, determination, and a hint of the unknown.

***

Under the relentless gaze of the sun and the comforting embrace of shade, through the dance of dust and the vibrant burst of bloom, King Sanjaya led his devoted retinue on an unwavering march spanning two months. Sixty leagues they traversed, a testament to the indomitable spirit of the kingdom.

Their journey culminated in the grand spectacle of Jetuttara's bustling gate, the city adorned in festive attire like a bride awaiting her groom. The air crackled with anticipation, and the entire realm transformed into a vibrant tapestry ablaze with the fire of expectation.

"Behold the grand return!" echoed through the streets, the town seemingly proclaiming its joy. The streets teemed with life, a choir singing songs and dances intertwining. Joy permeated the air, a palpable energy pulsating through the heart of the city.

From every nook and cranny, a multitude emerged, a chorus of elation rising like a symphony. Flags and handkerchiefs twirled high, their rhythmic dance synchronizing with the joyous beats of the heart.

Their Prince, their protector, their beloved son, arrived, embraced by the united gaze of his people. A celebration unfolded, a symphony of heartfelt praise echoing through the city. Songs and cheers became a triumphant chorus, ushering him through arches and walls that stood witness to the stories of generations.

With measured steps, King Sanjaya entered the heart of the palace, a sovereign's poise unfurling amidst the cheers and music. He reclaimed his throne, the ultimate pearl of his realm, marking the pinnacle of his triumphant return.

In this moment of reunion and exultant cheer, the tale unfolded gracefully, a chapter closing as destiny found its rightful place. The air shimmered with a sense of fulfillment, the homecoming echoing through the corridors of time as the kingdom embraced its sovereign. The characters' faces reflecting the journey's trials and victories bore witness to the culmination of a destiny intertwined with the very soul of Jetuttara.

***

The Great Being Vessantara, renowned for his boundless generosity and compassion, extended his kindness even to the smallest of creatures down to the humble cats that roamed the streets. As his chariot wheels rolled through the city gates, the scent of blooming flowers and the hum of excitement in the air enveloped him. A sense of anticipation lingered, like a finely woven tapestry of emotions waiting to be unfurled.

The night sky draped itself over the city, and the King pondered within the palace's hallowed chambers. The morrow would bring a procession of suitors, an assembly to honor his return. Amidst the flickering candlelight, his thoughts danced like the shadows on the walls. What gifts could he offer to match the joyous occasion? The weight of responsibility mingled with the warmth of anticipation.

As moonlight gently bathed his contemplative visage, a sudden realization unfurled. The throne beneath him seemed to emit a subtle warmth, a sensation that transcended the ordinary. He knew, in the depths of his being, that something divine was unfolding, something beyond the realm of mere mortals.

Sakka, the celestial ruler, witnessed this revealing moment from above. With an understanding that transcended time and space, he orchestrated a symphony of brilliance. The heavens opened, and like a cascade of stars, jewels of seven hues tumbled from the celestial realm. A deluge of precious gems, like a storm of blessings, descended upon the palace and the city beyond. The ground was adorned with their splendor, the palace grounds waist-deep in shimmering jewels, the city knee-deep in their radiant embrace.

The following day dawned, a tapestry woven with anticipation and hope. Families gathered, each with their hearts aflutter, drawn by the allure of treasures that had graced the earth. Like scattered dreams turned tangible, the jewels were shared among the people, passed from hand to hand and heart to heart. Vessantara, the embodiment of compassion, watched as his realm rejoiced in the abundance of the divine shower.

In the midst of this jubilation, as each gem found its home, the excess was carefully gathered. With reverence and foresight, they found their place within the treasury, a wellspring of generosity to sustain the kingdom's giving heart.

"Vessantara returned, a King with treasures rare,
A cascade of gold, a story beyond compare.
His gifts bestowed with love, his spirit laid to rest,
His wisdom echoed far, a legacy blessed."

A symphony of awe and realization rippled through the gathered assembly, a chorus of gratitude and understanding. Bound by the threads of a tale spun with wisdom, they marveled at the generosity that had unfolded before them, a great generosity that transcended time and touched the very core of their souls. Prince Vessantara's name became synonymous with compassion, his deeds woven into the very fabric of the kingdom's history.

***

Years passed, and the story of Prince Vessantara's great gifts was told and retold, inspiring future generations to live with open hearts and hands. The kingdom, once mired in strife and scarcity, became a beacon of hope and benevolence. And so, the tale of Prince Vessantara did not end with his passing but lived on, a shining example of the enduring power of love and generosity, forever guiding the hearts of those who heard it. The realm prospered, a living tribute to the King who taught them that true riches are found in the act of giving, and the greatest treasure is a heart full of love.

Publisher's Acknowledgement

This book features illustrative paintings curated from the esteemed collection of Wat Lao Samakkhidhammaram, Laval, QC. We express our deepest gratitude to the temple for allowing us to showcase these remarkable pieces of art.

UPCOMING BOOKS
by ASHIN SUMANACARA

THE ANIMAL PROTAGONISTS
50 Jataka Stories of Wisdom and Wonder

PSYCHOLOGICAL ASPECTS OF JATAKA STORIES
Exploring the Psychological Mysteries in Ancient Narratives

HEAVENLY PATHS
Stories of Merit and Virtue from the Vimanavatthu Commentary

PATHWAYS OF DHAMMA
Annotated Verses of the Dhammapada for Personal Growth and Spiritual Wellness

VIRTUOUS PATH, WEALTHY INSIGHTS
Illuminating Kural's Teachings on Dharma and Artha - A Literal Translation and Commentary

PUBLISHED BOOKS
by ASHIN SUMANACARA

MEANINGFUL LIFE, FEARLESS DEATH
Spiritual Insights on Death, Dying, Hospice Care and Grief Counseling

THE TALE OF PRINCE VESSANTARA
A Novel

About Subhashita Books

Subhashita Books publishes a diverse range of insightful literature that explores Eastern philosophy, self-help, mindfulness and spiritual teachings. To learn more about our offerings or to discuss publishing opportunities, please contact us.

SUBHASHITA BOOKS
3381 Boul Dagenais O.
Laval, QC, Canada
H7P IV5

Subhashita Books is affiliated with a non-profit organization and distributes published books and educational resources.